I sat up in the bed. Facing me was a heavy antique bureau. I could see myself dimly in the oval mirror above it. I saw I was nude above my waist. Slipping my hands beneath the quilt, I found I was nude entirely. I caressed my body languidly for a moment and felt vaguely aroused.

Suddenly, the door into the room opened quietly. And standing before me in the doorway was Selene. She wore a long, flowing robe seeming to be of that same almost transparent fabric which curtained the window. I gazed at her speechless, drinking in the loveliness of her as she stood there motionless, smiling at me. Her long pale hair and her body glowed in the moonlight streaming through the tall window. Her large dark eyes glittered above the flickering flame of the creamy-white candle she held.

I was overwhelmed by her beauty. I stared at her open-mouthed, amazed, enchanted.

She placed her candle on the bedside table. In silence she unfastened her sheer robe and dropped it to her feet. She bent toward me in her nude splendor. Trembling, I wrapped my arms around her slender waist and buried my face in her smooth, warm breasts, my eyes wet with tears of joy.

About the Author

Meredith More is a pseudonym. The author's real name happens to be the same as that of a well-known writer of lesbian fiction — not one as famous as Jane Rule, but an established writer with whom this author might be confused if she were to use that same name.

"Meredith" is a Tar Heel native who has lived, taught, and written in the Tidewater Area of Virginia since the sixties. She enjoys leisure time socializing with longtime friends and making new friends. She is currently writing her second novel.

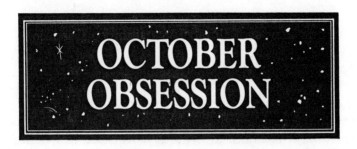

OCTOBER OBSESSION

BY MEREDITH MORE

NAIAD PRESS
1988

Printed in the United States of America
First Edition

Edited by Katherine V. Forrest
Cover design by Pat Tong and Bonnie Liss
    (Phoenix Graphics)
Typesetting by Sandi Stancil

Library of Congress Cataloging-in-Publication Data

More, Meredith, 1937—
    October obsession / by Meredith More.
        p.   cm.
    ISBN 0-941483-18-5
    I. Title.
PS3563.07718O28 1988   88-4859
813'.54--dc 19   CIP

DEDICATED WITH GRATITUDE TO

those who helped so much at each stage — Fay, who word-processed the semi-legible and ever-changing first draft; Charles, who encouraged me from day one and read every draft; Phyllis and Diane, whose insights during revisions of later drafts were particularly helpful; and finally, my outstanding editor, Katherine V. Forrest, whose coast-to-coast critiquing made possible this final draft. Thanks also to Barbara Grier and Naiad Press for publishing my first novel.

CHAPTER ONE
Friday, October 8, 1982

The sheriff's sandy-brown squad car was parked on the narrow shoulder of North Carolina Route 12 a few hundred feet north of the entrance to the Oregon Inlet bridge. Laura Westmoreland slowly pulled up behind it, the wheels of the rented silver-blue Mustang crunching on the oyster-shell gravel. She glanced at her watch. Almost four-thirty, Eastern time. His estimate had been precise. She ran a hand nervously through her short, dark

1

brown hair and squeezed the tight muscles at the base of her neck.

A tall, lean man dressed in a tan uniform emerged from the squad car. Laura rolled down her window as he approached, his tan jacket flapping in the brisk Atlantic breeze. She liked the fact that he was not wearing a pistol.

"Afternoon, ma'am." He tipped his black-billed tan cap and leaned toward her, smiling pleasantly. She recognized the soft drawl instantly. "I reckon you're Miz Westmoreland?" he continued, studying her face with gentle, pale blue eyes.

"Yes." She smiled politely.

"I'm Bill Tate." He offered a paw-like, weathered hand — tanned and slightly leathery, like his face. Laura guessed he was about a decade older than she, perhaps in his mid-forties. "I reckon we sort of know each other already," he added.

"Yes," she said, shaking his hand. "I guess we do." She had talked with him long distance four times in the last forty-eight hours. "Has anything . . . Have you found my aunt yet?"

"No, ma'am," he said softly. "Nothing's changed since you phoned a few hours back." Laura had telephoned him from Norfolk International Airport as soon as her plane from San Francisco had arrived. "We're still searching the island," Tate added. He coughed and looked away, toward the long narrow bridge leading to Hatteras Island. "Searching the waters too." He coughed again, then looked back at Laura. "Well, ma'am," he said in a somewhat brighter tone, "I reckon we'd best get on down the road."

"Thank you for meeting me here, Sheriff," Laura said. "After six years I just wasn't sure —"

"Quite all right, ma'am. My pleasure." He tipped his billed cap. "You're more'n welcome."

She watched him walk back to his squad car. From the moment he had first telephoned her on Wednesday afternoon with the news that her only living aunt, Josephine Westmoreland, had not been seen since Sunday, Laura had instinctively trusted and respected this total stranger. It was more than the kind, reassuring tone of his soft Carolinian drawl that assured her he would do everything possible to find Josie. It was also the fact that Sheriff Tate was obviously a Banker, as the natives of the Outer Banks called themselves. And Laura knew from Josie that Bankers cared deeply about their own.

Although a native of Richmond, Virginia, Josie had become a Banker decades ago, not simply by sharing the islanders' southern, Anglo-Saxon heritage, but by sharing too their values. Like them, Josie was proudly independent and self-reliant. Like them, she loved and respected the fragile environment of the long, narrow barrier islands forming half of the coastline of North Carolina, and she strongly resisted the outsiders who wanted to exploit the beauty of the Banks by filling the islands with high-rise hotels and fast food outlets.

Yes, Laura thought, watching Tate get into his car, this soft-spoken sheriff had to care about the fate of her Aunt Josie. Because this strong, self-sufficient woman of seventy who lived a simple, private life on remote Hatteras Island was one of his own — a Banker.

Laura followed Tate's car down the deserted two-lane highway and onto the bridge that snaked west, then south through the marshland, rose to a high hump over Oregon Inlet, then sloped southeast onto Hatteras. The gloomy grayness of the overcast late afternoon sky did not

3

diminish the beauty all about her, and despite her fears and fatigue she found the panoramic view as breathtakingly beautiful as she had remembered. She slowed at the high peak above the channel and looked back to the northeast at the tremendous expanse of creamy-white beach, totally deserted and shaped like an arrowhead, its Atlantic edge pounded by heavy breakers, its inlet edge lapped by gentle waves.

Due east at the wide, treacherous mouth of the inlet, slate blue whitecaps swept over a maze of half-submerged sandbars. West of her the waters of Roanoke Sound and Pamlico Sound converged in ever-shifting currents. The variegated blues and grays and light browns — and the patches wind-rippled or smooth — betrayed from this height the hidden sandbars and shallower channels that snaked into the narrow main channel of the inlet, which was deeper and dark blue.

A gorgeous expanse of water, Laura thought, but deadly too. Countless boats had been destroyed here, countless lives lost. She recalled Tate's words grimly: "Searching the waters too." No, she thought, shaking her head firmly. Not that. She stared at the approaching marshland, telling herself that Josie could not be dead, that she was simply lost, and that she herself, or Tate, would find her.

Leaving the bridge, Laura glanced back at it several times. The tall concrete pilings above the channel looked like spidery legs; the bridge itself seemed fragile, tentative, almost unreal as it receded into the distance. Like all things seemingly solid on the Outer Banks, it in fact rested, she knew, upon a bed of ever-shifting sand. The inlet it bridged had itself existed only about one hundred years. It had been created by a major hurricane.

4

The bridge had been built in the 1950s — after yet another major hurricane.

Looking at it one last time in the gray distance, Laura thought of the bridge now as a thin white umbilical cord. This bridge and three others — two of them linking Roanoke Island to the Banks and the mainland, the third across Currituck Sound north of Kitty Hawk — were the only solid life-supporting links between over three hundred miles of fragile, pencil-shaped islands and their mainland mother. And even this apparent solidity was tenuous, deceptive. A major hurricane could shred these concrete ribbons in a matter of hours. Laura marvelled again at Josie's choice of Hatteras Island for her home.

But as she followed Tate's car down the lonely highway, the pale yellow-white Atlantic dunes to her left, the marsh grasses and waters of Pamlico Sound to her right, she understood, even admired, Josie's decision to become a Banker. Between the undulating dunes topped by occasional clusters of sea oats — tall, thin yellow stalks nodding their heavy heads westward in the wind — and the narrow black-topped highway were thick stands of scrubby evergreen bushes. Laura smiled, spotting a red-winged blackbird atop a bayberry bush. She looked toward the sound and saw a v-shaped flock of Canada geese flying northward. This upper tip of the island, she remembered, was part of the national wildlife refuge that began south of Nags Head, ten miles or more north of Oregon Inlet. Except for the asphalt road and an occasional parking area with an observation stand, this area was untouched by human life. And Josie loved the wildlife here, and the solitude.

Thick forests of bayberry and yaupon holly soon obscured Laura's view of both the sound and the oceanfront dunes. Her mind returned to the events of the last two days, to the nagging awful question: Where was Josie?

Tate had reached Laura at the mental health clinic where she practiced family counseling. Her aunt, he said, had disappeared without a clue sometime after Sunday afternoon. He first became aware something was wrong purely by accident. Late Monday afternoon, near closing time at the local ice plant, the owner casually mentioned to Tate that his most faithful year-round customer for block ice had not shown up that day as she always did on Monday and Thursday mornings. Tate knew who he meant from the description — "That elderly lady who lives all to herself up around Rodanthe."

Thinking the lady might be ill or injured, Tate drove up to her cottage. Her Ford station wagon was there, doors locked and windows closed; both doors to the cottage were bolted, and every window was shuttered and locked. "I knocked and yelled, ma'am," Tate told Laura, "but nobody answered. It didn't look right to me, the place all locked up but the wagon still there. And she hadn't missed a Monday morning at the ice plant in at least ten years, Joe said." Finally he broke into the house. "Uneasy about her," he said, "given her age." No one was there and nothing looked disturbed, inside or outside the small oceanfront cottage. "No signs of violence," he reassured Laura, "but I felt I oughtta look into it."

By Wednesday morning he had organized search parties. And that afternoon, he contacted Laura.

After a sleepless night, Laura telephoned him early Thursday. She had to do something. She felt she could not merely sit there in San Francisco and wait. She would fly to Norfolk as soon as possible and rent a car at the airport.

Tate sounded pleased, even grateful. "I could surely use your help, ma'am," he said. "Your personal knowledge of the house, and of your aunt."

Her colleagues at the clinic were sympathetic and helpful. Dr. Leah Stein, her supervisor, insisted Laura take as long a leave as necessary. "She's like a mother to you, I know," she said. "Don't worry. We'll handle your appointments, reschedule where we can." She knew Laura's parents were dead and that Laura was closely attached to her only living aunt. Several other counselors offered to help. And even the normally reticent secretary, dour-faced Madge, had spoken to Laura kindly and had volunteered to book her flight.

Tate's car slowed from fifty-five to forty-five, then forty, thirty-five. Laura tensed and gnawed her lower lip, lightly braking the Mustang and scanning the low bushes and pale dunes to the east. A tan and brown Winnebago impatiently passed the two cars and sped on down the arrow-straight road. Maryland plates, dozens of decals, surf-fishing rods lashed to the rear. Laura envied the occupants' holiday eagerness.

Tate's left turn signal blinked. The squad car slowed to twenty-five, twenty. Through the scrubby bushes she saw the wood-shingled roof. She followed Tate's car into the narrow gray-white driveway of crushed oyster shells, ending this long journey she had dreaded making, yet had had to make. Perhaps her final journey to Josie's home.

Laura's eyes riveted immediately on the light blue 1972 Ford station wagon parked beneath the small house that stood upon thick round pilings like telephone poles, blackened and creosoted — pilings visible only from this back side of the cottage. From the oceanfront side, Laura remembered, Josie's wood-shingled home appeared to sit on top of a sand dune.

Tate carried Laura's red suitcase in one hand, a large flashlight in the other. Laura followed him up the steep, weathered stairs and onto the narrow wooden porch running the length of the back of the cottage. "Had no choice, ma'am," he said apologetically, shaking his head. "Had to shoot out the deadbolt."

"That's all right. I understand," she said reassuringly, noticing the shiny new padlock above the gaping hole.

He gestured toward the windows, covered by heavy wooden shutters. "It was either a door or a window," he continued, pulling a large key ring from his jacket. "Would of made a worse mess with the glass." He searched through the keys.

Laura hugged herself against the chilling wind, wishing she had worn something warmer than her blue business suit and thin white turtleneck sweater. She looked from Tate to the western vista. Pale, gently-rolling sand; spiky, wind-swept grass. The thick stand of bayberry bushes edging the highway. Across the road, a wide band of dark, green-gray bushes. And then, like a slate gray ribbon, Pamlico Sound, its horizon barely visible now against the darkening gray sky. Ten miles or more between this spot and the mainland, she remembered.

She turned toward the muffled thunder of the ocean's surf and looked south along the wind-swept crests of the yellow-white dunes, graying now in the gathering dusk. Thin clumps of sea oats and hair-thin grass bowed westward in the wind. Between the dunes she glimpsed the dark Atlantic.

Tate opened the door, picked up Laura's suitcase, and switched on his flashlight. Still hugging her arms, Laura followed him down the dark narrow hallway that led past

8

the kitchen and into the living room. The boarded-up cottage was very cold.

Tate placed her suitcase beside the worn blue velvet couch and removed his cap. He pointed his flashlight at a kerosene lantern suspended from a beam above the marble-topped coffee table. "Reckon you recollect there's no electricity, ma'am," he said.

"Yes, I know." She dropped her shoulder bag onto the light gray table and sat down wearily on the couch. She picked up a blue and white afghan and threw it around her shoulders, watching Tate light the lantern. Then she studied the room, now bathed in pale light. Everything looked as she had remembered.

Facing the couch were the two tall, wide-paned windows. Behind the glass were the wide-planked vertical shutters. Hair-thin streaks of gray daylight broke the boards. Between the twin windows sat as always the small round cherrywood table holding a cream-colored candle and small box of matches. The faded, pale blue drapes were drawn back from the windows. She could not recall ever seeing them closed.

Left and right of the windows stood the familiar matching oak bookcases — tall, heavy Victorian pieces. Behind their wood-framed glass doors she could dimly see Josie's treasures — old leather bound books, the family Bible, seashells, driftwood, pieces of china and silver. And the framed pictures of family members, most of them long dead. Was Josie dead now too? Laura shivered slightly, shook her head, denying this awful thought.

"Miz Westmoreland," said Tate, "how about I build a little fire for you?" He nodded toward the black iron woodstove which stood on a gray marble slab before the sealed-off fireplace on the south wall.

"That would be very nice, yes," she said, hugging the afghan to her. "Thank you."

He chatted across the room as he built the fire. "Crazy weather this time of year. One day you're running the air conditioning. Next day — building a fire!" He chuckled and dusted his big hands lightly on his trousers, peering into the black stove. "Oughtta leave this lid off for a while," he said, "till she gets going good." He glanced at Laura and smiled pleasantly, running a hand through his thick, lightly graying hair.

"Thank you," Laura said, moving toward the stove. She held her hands out, warming them.

Tate gestured to the shuttered windows. "How about I open these storm windows for you, ma'am . . . while there's still some daylight left?"

Laura hesitated. He had done so much for her already.

"Tell you what, Miz Westmoreland," he said, zipping up his jacket. "Back there in the kitchen there's ground coffee and all the fixings. How about I take care of the windows, and you fix us some good black coffee?"

"You've got a deal, Sheriff."

"Oh . . . and would you unlatch the bolts for me, ma'am?"

"Certainly."

Laura opened the bolts on the living room windows, then started toward Josie's bedroom. But she paused at the mahogany roll-top desk against the north wall. On either side of the brass oil lamp atop the desk, in matching gold frames, stood the familiar high school graduation portraits of herself and her only cousin, Larry. She smiled at their teenaged faces.

Larry in 1964 . . . eighteen years ago. His blue-gray mortarboard tilted jauntily. A confident, almost cocky grin on his wide mouth. His deep brown eyes almost

10

laughing. His dark brown hair worn in the style of the Beatles: long sideburns, bangs brushing his eyebrows.

They had grown up together on the same street in Richmond. She used to pretend he was her brother. They looked like brother and sister, with the same dark brown hair with a hint of chestnut, thick and slightly wavy, and the same Westmoreland chin — the lower face tapering almost into a Valentine shape.

What a radical he had been, marching in protests against the undeclared war in Vietnam, wearing ragged jeans, letting his hair flow down to his shoulders. But now — Major Lawrence S. Westmoreland, Jr., U.S. Army career officer, husband, father of three children. How abruptly his life had changed. Within a year after his graduation from William and Mary, he had joined the Army. What had motivated him? Desperation? Some buried need for self-punishment? He had long since stopped confiding in Laura. Somewhat sadly Laura looked away from the picture of the youthful Larry. She still loved him like a brother, but their relationship had leveled, years ago, into the superficial. She rarely saw him now.

Laura looked at the 1965 portrait of herself. How stiff and proper she looked in her slate-blue cap and gown, her mortarboard sitting perfectly level. She smiled at the bouffant hairdo — permed, teased, sprayed to Brillo-pad stiffness. The smile was tense, almost forced. Pride, joy . . . fear. How elated, yet terrified, she had been, preparing to enter the University of Virginia. Not yet eighteen, wanting to be a mature woman, yet fearing it. Taking with her to the university her collection of stuffed animals.

How proud Josie had always been of her and Larry. Proud of Laura's degrees in psychology, her career as a counselor. Proud too of Larry's promotions in rank. Laura smiled, remembering Josie's defense of Larry during his radical phase. When his hair had reached the shoulder-length stage, Josie had said to his father — her brother — "Never mind, Lawrence, what's growing *on* his skull. It's what's growing *beneath* it that matters."

Aware of dull gray daylight, Laura turned to find one of the twin windows unshuttered. She saw Tate on the porch, moving a short wooden ladder toward the second window. She went quickly into the kitchen, filled the copper teakettle, and placed it on the kerosene stove.

Hearing a loud rapping at the shuttered window, she raced back through the living room and into Josie's bedroom. Quickly she raised the lower sash and unbolted the heavy shutter. As Tate opened it, a stiff wind whipped the gossamer curtains. Tate descended the ladder and looked at her through the half-opened window. "That does it for the front ones," he said above the thundering of the surf. "Be ready for that hot cup of coffee in about five minutes." He and the ladder disappeared.

Laura closed the window and went into the room behind the bedroom, which Josie called The Closet. It housed an odd assortment — furniture, cardboard boxes, even Josie's fishing rods and tackle. In one corner sat the two extra chairs to the oak kitchen table; in another, the two heavy white rocking chairs that in warm weather sat on the beachfront porch. Among the bookcases, trunks, chairs and boxes in The Closet, only one thing was free of dust — Josie's gray metal desk facing the window. Sitting on it, neatly covered, was the old manual typewriter.

Laura unlatched the bolts to the window in this room, then the small window in the bathroom, which was dominated by a large, claw-footed white bathtub. Then she returned to the kitchen. Unlatching the two shutters there, she thought again about Josie's strange disappearance, remembering the station wagon parked beneath the kitchen, just under her feet. Five days now . . . Could Josie still be alive? She had to be. But where was she? Why had she left the car? Laura's hand shook slightly as she scooped coffee grounds into the Dripolator.

Returning to the living room, Laura poked absently at the fire in the iron stove, slipped the round black lid half over it. Warm now, she removed her blue suit jacket, draped it over an arm of the couch. She pulled off her pumps and flexed her toes, then walked across the oriental rug to the oceanfront windows. Twilight was approaching. Less than a hundred yards distant, the blackening Atlantic pounded the smooth beach with never-ceasing thunder muffled by the closed windows.

The wide beach was deserted except for an occasional gull. The sea oats on the low dune rising up to Josie's cottage bowed toward her in the wind. How beautiful, how peaceful, she thought. Jackie would love this island . . . would be snapping pictures day by night. Laura smiled, imagining Jackie there with her cameras, tripod, countless rolls of film . . . But why was she again thinking of Jackie? Laura shook her head sadly.

The tea kettle began whistling just as Tate knocked at the back door. Laura raced to let him in, then rushed to remove the shrieking kettle. When she joined Tate a few minutes later in the living room, he was poking at the fire, his jacket draped over the back of the Morris chair. He asked if she minded if he smoked a cigarette.

"Not at all," she said, handing him a steaming mug of black coffee. "You can use the seashell on the coffee table for an ashtray." She sat down on the couch, cradling her mug of coffee.

13

He pulled a pack of Salems from his shirt pocket, sat in the Morris chair, tapped his fingers nervously on the chair arm. "Miz Westmoreland," he said, leaning forward, "I know you must be plumb worn out. Traveling all day, making that two-hour drive down here from Norfolk." He coughed, cleared his throat. "So if you ain't up to it right now, we can discuss the case tomorrow, ma'am. After you've rested."

"Oh I want to discuss it now," she said, folding her arms and looking at him expectantly.

He stroked his lightly stubbled chin. "It's a real puzzlement, ma'am. But some facts are clear." He paused to sip his coffee. "No forced entry — except mine. All the fingerprints your aunt's. No blood, no signs of struggle . . . She didn't surprise a burglar and get herself hurt or killed for it —"

"But maybe kidnapped by him?" Laura interrupted, leaning forward.

"Not likely." He shook his head. "Surprised burglars don't kidnap people. They knock them out, or kill them, or just flee. But let's suppose you were such a burglar, and decided to take this elderly lady with you . . . maybe to kill her someplace else." He looked at Laura thoughtfully. "Would you do all this, and yet not rob the place?"

She hesitated. "No. I guess a burglar would take something." She looked at the undisturbed pieces of silver and china in the bookcases facing her, remembered the china and crystal in the kitchen's corner cabinet. "Nothing's missing, as far as I've noticed."

He got up and paced. "You'd know that better'n I would, Miz Westmoreland. So you can help me there. Check every room real carefully. Maybe there is something missing. Like jewelry."

Laura smiled. "Not jewelry," she said. "Josie has little interest in jewelry. Gave me the few family pieces she had, years ago."

"Did she collect something valuable — like coins, antique clocks?"

Laura shook her head, looked at him. "Clocks? Whatever made you think of clocks?" she asked with a little laugh.

"There ain't a clock in this house." He shrugged. "The only obvious thing that's missing."

"Well, that's because Josie hates them," she explained. "After she retired from the post office in Richmond, Josie gave away every clock she owned. Her watches, too." Laura pointed to her wrist. "This gold Bulova, it's Josie's. Once she moved to Hatteras," she continued, "Josie said the only clock she needed was the one inside her body, and the sun and the moon."

Tate faced her, his hands in his pockets. "Miz Westmoreland, whatever happened to your aunt, it didn't happen here, inside the house. Nothing missing, no fingerprints —"

"Maybe someone wearing gloves?" She rubbed her neck, trying to relieve her tension. "A kidnapper, not a thief?"

"No ma'am." He shook his head firmly. "Remember the bolted shutters, and the deadbolts on both doors . . . If you were such a kidnapper, or thief . . . Would you take twenty minutes of precious time to get out the ladder, shutter all the windows, come back inside, bolt them all down . . ." He paused. "It just didn't happen here. I'm sure of it."

Laura stared at him. So very logical, so observant, so thorough. Beneath the homespun manner was a painstakingly careful investigator. She admired him.

15

"Yes," she said, "you're right. It could not have happened here."

He returned to the Morris chair, put out his Salem. "No ma'am, I don't think so," he said softly. He leaned forward, his paw-like hands on his thighs. "She battened down the hatches herself, and then walked off . . . under her own will."

"And ran into some maniac," Laura said bitterly.

"No ma'am. I highly doubt that. I can't find no motive here for homicide."

"Psychopathic killers don't have to have motives," she said somewhat coldly. "Not from what we understand, anyway."

"Yes ma'am, I know," he said gently. "But you see . . . This time of year, there's hardly anybody out here but us Bankers. And I reckon I know my people pretty well. Ain't a resident of this island I don't know by sight if not name. Decent, hard-working people. We got a few bad eggs, like everybody, but not any bad enough to kill an elderly lady for no reason."

He went to the stove, added a small log. "Most people on Hatteras are watermen, you know — out working the water twelve hours a day or more, all year. Fishing, crabbing, oystering." He replaced the lid over the fire and dusted his hands. "Some of them get a little rowdy when they're drinking. A few of them beat up sometimes on their wives." He looked at Laura. "But I can't think of a one of them that'd lay a hand on a white-haired lady of seventy. Not one."

"Maybe it wasn't a Banker," Laura said. "Someone from the mainland. Maybe an escaped criminal."

Tate chuckled. "There ain't no outsider on this island that don't get noticed, at least after the tourist season."

16

"It's possible she's just visiting with someone, some friend I don't know." She paused. "I know the station wagon's here, but still, isn't it possible?" She picked nervously at her skirt.

"Possible, but not very likely. She wasn't one for leaving the island much. When she did leave, she took her car."

"Well maybe something's wrong with the car —"

"Nothing's wrong with it." He looked at her sympathetically. "I checked it out myself. And you know there's no buses out here, no taxicabs, trains, planes . . ." He held up a hand. "Wait here just a minute, please . . . There's another fact."

He disappeared into Josie's bedroom, returned quickly with a brown leather purse. Handing it to Laura he said, "Found it just this morning, with three other purses. Top shelf of the wardrobe."

Laura looked at the purse, her face paling slightly.

"Please open it, ma'am" he said.

One by one she removed the billfold, the coin purse, the comb, the checkbook, the car keys — even Josie's reading glasses were there.

He coughed. "Twenty-three dollars in the wallet. About two dollars more in the change purse."

Laura numbly returned each item to the purse. She felt as if some heavy fist had been rammed into her stomach. She looked up at Tate, her eyes moist. "Please be honest. Tell me, please . . . where do you think she is?"

His pale blue eyes were sympathetic. He nodded toward the oceanfront windows. "Out there, he said softly. "I'm mighty much afraid, ma'am, that your aunt's out there . . . in the water."

Laura shivered, hearing the muffled pounding of the waves. "It can't be," she said, shaking her head firmly. "It can't."

"I'm sorry, ma'am," he said gently, "but it's the best theory I got . . . And I'm afraid it's gonna prove to be true."

"She couldn't swim," Laura said in a flat tone. "She was afraid of the water! She loved it, but she never went in more than knee deep." Laura thought of the many times she had surf-fished with Josie.

He nodded. "I know that. Didn't own a boat either, and nobody can recollect ever seeing her in one."

Laura studied his face. "Then how could she drown?"

"We don't call that stretch out there The Graveyard of the Atlantic for nothing . . . strong currents, bad ones. She might of been surf-casting, or just wading. It was in the high eighties Sunday." He paused, rubbed his chin. "Full moon too . . . I reckon you know how the moon affects the tides."

"It makes them go in and out." She shrugged.

"More than that." He nodded with emphasis. "The fuller the moon, the higher the tides, and the stronger. Full moon, you get the highest and strongest tide of the month."

"Wouldn't Josie know that?" She stood, walked toward the windows, stared at the dark gray sky and sea.

"Well, probably. But you know, old folks — sometimes they get forgetful."

Laura turned, smiled. "Not Josie! She is — was — just incredible! When I was here last, she almost wore me out." She laughed. "I'm half her age, yet I was the one with leg cramps from all that walking we did." She looked at him steadily. "As for her mind, her memory — very sharp, very alert."

18

"But that was six years ago, ma'am."

Laura folded her arms. "I've seen her since. In Norfolk, in Hampton. And we write often. She phones me at least once a month, from a pay telephone, in Rodanthe, I think." Laura paused. "She had cancer three years ago, but recovered completely. Her health is — was — excellent. Superior, even."

Tate walked toward her. "But sickness, physical or mental, it can come on sudden-like sometimes." He paused, lit a Salem, stared at the sea. "Like my Uncle Rhett. Amazing man, kinda like your aunt, I reckon. Was still working his boat at seventy-eight. Came in off the sound one afternoon, unloaded his flounder, started walking toward his pickup . . . Then, wham!" Tate snapped his fingers. "Just like that! Hit the ground, dead. Heart attack." He shook his head.

It was possible, Laura thought. "So maybe Josie," she said thoughtfully, "wading, or fishing . . . maybe a stroke, heart attack . . ." She looked at Tate.

"Possible, ma'am, yes. And then the moon tide —"

"Swept out to sea," she said softly. The clouds were breaking. A few stars were visible. The half-full moon drifted out from behind a cloud.

Tate coughed, cleared his throat. "There's some puzzling things, though," he said. "Like why she battened down the windows . . . no storm in sight." Laura turned to him, startled. "And like why she left this, over there on the coffee table." He pulled an index card from his back pocket and handed it to Laura.

"It's mine," said Laura, glancing at it. "I mailed it to her recently." She remembered the painful decision to move out of her apartment, in the same building as Jackie's, to relocate in another section of San Francisco.

"My new address and phone number. I moved about three weeks ago."

"Then I reckon maybe she had it out there on the table because she was planning to write you, or phone you."

"Why else?" She turned from him, looked again at the breaking clouds and the spangles of moonlight on the black waves, wishing that strong, confident Jackie were there with her to help ease her anxiety.

She heard Tate walk to the stove, lift the lid, poke at the fire. "When's the last time, Miz Westmoreland, you talked to your aunt?"

Laura shrugged. "Oh, maybe a month ago, early September. Yes, about a week after my birthday. She phoned to say she'd received the picture I sent, the one of me on her bedroom dresser."

"And how did she seem to you then?"

She looked at him, wondering what he was thinking. "Well, just . . . just like Josie, like herself. She was happy, excited about the picture." Laura walked back to the couch. "It was a late birthday present to her, one she requested."

"I see. Didn't sound depressed? Or a little confused?"

"No! Not at all! Are you implying she might have been . . . suicidal?" She stared at him wide-eyed.

He coughed. "No ma'am, not exactly that. But the mental health, you know . . . like the physical, sometimes it can go, right sudden-like." He paced the rug before her.

Laura said tactfully, "I believe someone in my profession would be able to recognize certain signs —"

"Oh yes ma'am!" he interrupted, nodding. "That's one reason I was so glad you offered to come here — because I knew you'd be able to help me there."

20

She leaned back into the couch, folded her arms. "So you feel some possibility Josie was not her usual self when she disappeared?"

"Well, I been thinking a lot lately about my Aunt Flo. Never knew a smarter woman. Kept up with everything, had a memory like a filing cabinet. Real alert, just like your aunt. Then one evening, she told Uncle Harry — that's her husband — that she knew he was intending to kill her, and run off with this young girl at the post office. Said the little people in the TV set had crawled right out of there and told her."

Hands stuffed in his pockets, Tate stopped pacing and looked at Laura. "Just a few weeks more, Aunt Flo didn't even know who Uncle Harry was. Kept saying he was the Devil, come to carry her off to Hell. Things like that." He sighed. "So, you never can tell, can you, when the mental health might go?"

"It's rare," she replied, "a case like your aunt's ... but yes, it can happen." She couldn't believe, however, that it could have happened to Josie. She sighed and squeezed her shoulders, suddenly feeling quite fully the weariness of her day's ordeal.

"Almost six now, ma'am," he said. "I know you're tired. Maybe I'd best leave now, come back tomorrow."

"If you don't mind, if you have the time," she said, "I'd like to hear first your reasons why you think Josie might have been ill, perhaps even suicidal." She picked up the empty coffee mugs. "But maybe your wife's waiting —"

"Dinner ain't until seven for her and me." He chuckled. "She feeds the teenagers first, so we can have some peace and quiet."

Noticing an unlabeled bottle of white wine on the kitchen table, the home-made wine Josie always had,

Laura called out, "Are you allowed to have a glass of wine?"

Tate chuckled as she brought in the bottle and glasses. "Well, officially, my day ends at five-thirty, so I reckon it's all right." He uncorked the bottle, poured each of them a glass. "It's mighty good," he observed after a few sips.

"Some friend of Josie's makes it, a young woman, I believe. I've never met her." Laura sipped her wine. "Now tell me why you believe Josie was not herself when she disappeared."

"Well, first, the shutters. Then too, that index card. It was like maybe it was left on purpose, for me to find — almost, you see, a suicide note. Like she wanted me to be sure to notify her next of kin."

Laura shook her head. "No, I think she was planning to write me, or telephone. But it is strange about the shutters, yes."

"Now, the ice box is bone dry and empty, like she wouldn't be needing it anymore. But the pantry — it's well stocked. A whole lot of canned goods, a dozen bottles or more of this white wine. And a lot of fresh foods — potatoes, carrots, onions, fruits like apples and oranges." He leaned back in his chair. "Question is, was this food meant for her? Or did she leave it here for you?"

Laura looked at him with a furrowed brow. "I still don't see, except for the windows —"

"Here's the truly strange part, ma'am," he interrupted. "The way she was behaving the last time anybody saw her." He leaned forward. "Sunday afternoon, Skeeter Thomas — they call him Skeeter 'cause he's so long-legged and skinny, like a mosquito — he was out on the beach less than half a mile south of here. Acting as a fishing guide for a small party, half a

22

dozen government boys, down from D.C., surf-fishing for blues — bluefish, you know."

Laura nodded, remembering that this sport fish migrated along the Outer Banks in the spring and fall months.

"Your aunt, Skeeter says, came walking down the beach, and motioned him over to her. It was around about four-thirty. Skeeter was kinda surprised. They knew each other by sight, you see, but . . . Well, your aunt, she was always kind of a loner. Always kept to herself."

"Somewhat shy, yes," Laura agreed. "Except with the family."

"First time she'd ever done more than nod at Skeeter, he says," Tate continued. "And she had a particular request to make. A kind of peculiar request. She said something like this: 'Please don't let your fishing party move up toward my place. I'm afraid they might ruin the drawings.' Skeeter says she acted real tense, real worried. Like it was a matter of life or death to her. Like the world would come to an end if anybody stepped on or messed up some things she'd drawn in the sand up here near her house."

Tate leaned back in the chair, frowned slightly. "Well, Skeeter humored her; he's a good boy. Promised to keep the men away. Told her they were about to call it a day anyhow. So she thanked him and left. He watched her walk back on up the beach to her place."

Tate rubbed his chin. "Skeeter's always been kinda nosey. He wanted to see what was so all-fired important about those drawings in the sane. So about half an hour later he moseyed on up this way, to take a look."

Laura leaned forward, following this story with interest, wondering what it meant. "What had she drawn?"

"According to him, and I got no reason to disbelieve him, it was a long row of small circles. Perfect circles, near as he could judge." Tate finished his wine. "A straight line of circles, like a path. Started at the foot of her beach steps, ended near the edge of the surf. Twenty, thirty circles, maybe more. He didn't count them. Didn't touch them either."

Laura frowned. She could not remember Josie's ever having drawn anything at all in the sand.

"That's not all." He looked at Laura. "Each circle had drawings inside of it. Must of taken her hours. Skeeter says he couldn't make out most of it. He did recollect there was some moons . . . like crescent moons and halfmoons. A lot of the marks didn't make no sense to him at all. Kinda like letters, he says, but not in English."

Laura slowly shook her head, traced the moist rim of her wine glass with a finger. "Circles," she said softly. She looked up at Tate. "And you're sure this Skeeter person didn't make up this story? Perhaps to get attention?"

"I highly doubt it, ma'am. He ain't the type to pull jokes, make up wild stories. Don't have much imagination, you see." Tate shrugged and pulled out his pack of Salems. "Well, it might mean something; it might not. A lot of people like to draw in the sand."

But not Josie, she thought, concerned. She finished her wine silently, then said to Tate, "If Josie did this, I'd have to call it not typical of her. But I don't know . . . six years . . . Eccentric behavior, perhaps."

Tate shifted uneasily in his chair. "Some are calling it more than eccentric, ma'am. Especially the insurance people."

She looked at him, puzzled. "Insurance people?"

"I reckon then you don't know, ma'am, about the policies?"

She shrugged. "Well, I know there's some modest life insurance, the civil service policy, but —"

"Much more than that, Miz Westmoreland." He got up and beckoned her toward the roll-top desk. He opened the desk, picked up a packet of rubber-banded documents. "It's all right here. The will's on top, all proper and legal."

Laura was dumbfounded, amazed by the extent of Josie's estate. Tate pointed out each document: two large life insurance policies in addition to the civil service policy, an accidental death policy paying $200,000 — but not, Tate pointed out, if death was by suicide. There were also records of savings certificates, stocks, bonds.

"Not counting this," Tate said, gesturing around the room, "or even the beachfront property, about two city blocks of it out there, those papers you're holding right there represent, I'd say, over half a million dollars."

Laura stared open-mouthed at him. "But how?" It's not possible! She was only a postal clerk!" She felt almost light-headed.

Tate gently took back the bundle of documents, placed them in the desk, closed it. He touched her shoulder. "I reckon you'd best go sit back down, ma'am," he said softly. "You look kinda pale." He led her to the couch, poured a second glass of wine for her, none for himself.

"I just can't believe it," Laura said. "Her post office salary ... that little civil service pension."

"She lived on a shoestring, you know, real thrifty. No fancy things, no electrical bills. Biggest expense was probably the firewood — has to be brought out from the mainland, you know."

"All those years," Laura said softly. "Living in this simple way . . . yet building up a fortune." She stared blankly before her.

"All for you, ma'am," Tate said, pacing the rug. "And for her nephew, the Major." He paused. "Most of it goes to you. The house here and the land, and all the personal property. The rest, the insurance money, stocks and things, half to you, half to Major Westmoreland."

Laura took a big swallow from her glass of wine. "I still can't believe — Does Larry know this?"

"Oh yes, ma'am! I telephoned him today, at his base over in Germany." Tate smiled. "He couldn't believe it either, said there had to be some kind of mistake. You know, I've called him every day since Wednesday, just like you."

Laura nodded. "You've been very, very kind, Sheriff Tate, to both of us. And I appreciate it."

He flushed slightly. "Well, just doing my job." He looked at his watch. "Six-thirty almost. I'd best be going along home now."

Laura stood up. "Those insurance investigators," she said, "do they really believe it was suicide?" She shook her head. "I still can't believe —"

"Well, you know, their job is to save the company money," he said. "Not to pay off any policy if they can get out of it."

"Do you believe it? That Josie killed herself?"

"I don't know yet. But I kinda doubt it." He paused, scratched his chin. "It's that fear of hers, you see. The fear of drowning. Don't make sense to me that if she was going to kill herself, she'd do it that way."

Laura nodded. "No, it doesn't make sense." She felt somewhat relieved.

26

"Well, we'll keep looking." He shrugged. "But the chances are pretty slim at this point, ma'am. Not likely we'll ever recover her body," he said sympathetically.

Laura sighed, looked toward the beachfront windows. "It had to be an accident . . . I hope she didn't suffer much."

"I hope not too. Those insurance people, Miz Westmoreland, I think you ought to know this part too." He coughed.

By now she knew that his nervous coughs signaled unpleasant news. What else could there be, she wondered.

"They'll do their best, ma'am, to prove suicide, or probable suicide." He coughed again. "But if they can't make that stick, well . . . they ain't above going after you, ma'am. And the Major. Or both of you."

Laura's jaw dropped. "What do you mean?"

"They might try to prove that one of you, or the two of you together, had a hand in this disappearance. For the money."

"How . . . How could *anybody!*" Her voice rose with shock and anger. "That's totally —"

"Not possible," he finished. "I assure you, *I* don't believe it." He looked directly into her eyes. "Miz Westmoreland," he said gently, "I'm just telling you what those insurance vultures might try. But it won't wash, just won't wash at all."

"Indeed it won't," she said firmly.

"Too much evidence on your side," he said. "And the Major's."

"Evidence?" she asked, puzzled.

He grinned. "Yes ma'am, evidence of love." He pointed toward the roll-top desk. "Them pictures over there, for instance. This whole house is full of you and him and his family. Pictures everywhere. Letters. Bundles

27

of letters, all tied up with ribbons. Letters from you, and him. Picture albums too."

Laura smiled and nodded. "Josie always saved every little thing. Even the drawings we did as children."

"Looking at it logically, what would be the motive? And the means? The Major's in Germany, you're in California. One, or both, of you, would have to hire somebody, pay somebody to come out here, kill her, get rid of the body." He shook his head.

Laura smiled with effort. "A scenario right out of a movie."

He shrugged. "And what would be the motive?"

Laura chuckled ironically. "The money, of course."

"Which, number one, you didn't know about, either of you. I'm convinced of that." He picked up his cap and flashlight. "And which, number two, you don't desperately need, not bad enough to kill for it — both of you've got good credit ratings, no heavy debts, no problems like gambling or drugs." He paused, coughed. "I, uh, had to check on you both, ma'am, just routine."

"Of course," she said. "I understand."

"And third," he said, "is her age. In the natural course of things, you'd be inheriting this estate soon anyway. So why would either of you take a chance on losing it all?"

She held out her hand. He shook it and said, "You get some rest now, eat something, ma'am. I'll check in with you tomorrow, around lunchtime." He adjusted his cap. "And I do hope you'll go over the house very carefully, in case there's something missing. Or anything out of the ordinary."

"Yes, I will," she said.

After he left she carried her suitcase into Josie's bedroom and quickly changed into pajamas, slippers and a robe. It felt good to free her body from the constricting underwear, the panty hose.

She went into the kitchen, stared blankly at the shelves in the panty, decided she was too tired to eat. She went back into the living room, added a small log to the fire and finished her glass of wine.

She stretched out on the worn couch, pulling an afghan over her, meaning to rest for a while, then eat something. Almost instantly she fell into a deep sleep.

CHAPTER TWO
Saturday, October 9

A dazzling sunrise awoke Laura. She got up groggily to close the drapes against the fiery red-gold rays, then quickly changed her mind. This brilliant sunrise, breaking the deep blue-purple of sky and sea, rivaled all the spectacular Pacific sunsets she had ever seen. She stoked the stove, pulled the Morris chair to the windows, wrapped herself in the afghan, and curled up to enjoy the shifting patterns of colors that streaked the sky and danced upon the undulating waves. How many hundreds of such sunrises had Josie witnessed here? And had she willingly chosen to leave them?

As dawn gave way to day, Laura left the windows, quite hungry after her dinnerless evening. Black coffee, two oranges, apple slices spread thickly with peanut butter — she had almost forgotten how good such a simple fruit meal could taste.

After donning jeans, a warm red sweater and running shoes, she began a methodical search of the cottage. She would prove to herself, if not to Tate, how impossible the suicide theory was.

She began with the bedroom. Everything looked the same. Josie's heavy four-poster mahogany bed was neatly covered, as usual, with a patchwork quilt. The three old suitcases stored beneath the bed were empty. The antique bedside table held an oil lamp and a book — *Ghost Stories and Legends of the Outer Banks.* The table's drawers contained such ordinary odds and ends as a flashlight, matches, scissors, needles and thread, a nail file.

She examined next the massive Victorian walnut dresser facing the bed. Suspended above it was the familiar walnut-framed oval mirror, and on top of the dresser studio portraits of Laura and Josie. Laura smiled at the gilt Victorian frame Josie had chosen for the recent picture of her. The old photograph of Josie Laura had not seen for decades. The date 1947 was inked into a corner.

How strange to see Josie and herself both at age thirty-five. Laura was struck by the strong resemblance. She had always known she had Josie's eyes — violet-blue with long dark lashes — but the younger Josie's hair was like hers too, dark brown with chestnut highlights. No wonder people had often mistaken them for mother and daughter.

31

The deep heavy drawers held nothing unusual. Gloves, socks, neatly folded stacks of underwear, pajamas, sweaters. She found this orderliness reassuring, a reflection of Josie's practicality, her sanity.

Orderly too was the ornately carved cherrywood wardrobe that loomed to the right of the room's single window. Laura went through everything hanging in it, checking the pockets of coats, jackets, jeans and slacks. She shook every shoe and boot. She examined every purse and box on the shelves. She stared uncomfortably at the brown leather purse Tate had handed her to inspect the night before.

Finally she examined the huge oak trunk to the left of the window. The cedar-lined trunk, handmade by Josie's father, held the usual linens, blankets, quilts. Laura removed each piece, shook it, refolded it. Then she neatly returned everything and closed the lid.

Her two-hour search of this bedroom had yielded nothing, absolutely nothing, to explain Josie's disappearance — or her death . . . if indeed Josie was dead. Why could she not yet believe Tate's theory?

Wearied by conflicting emotions of hope and despair, Laura sat down heavily on the edge of the bed. For a moment she stared absently at the old oil painting facing her. Then, realizing she had never seen it before, she examined it curiously. At the bottom of the elaborately carved frame was a small bronze label: *Cynthia and Endymion.*

One of the two figures was a pale, almost ethereal woman with long blonde hair. She was barefoot, and dressed in a thin, flowing gown that blew lightly in the wind. Suspended above her head was a full moon, bathing her and the other figure in soft moonlight. The woman was looking lovingly, almost pensively, at a handsome young man in a Grecian toga and sandals, who was peacefully sleeping at her feet. His head, covered in thick brown ringlets, was cradled in one arm; the other arm, extended before him, rested at the edge of a perfect circle drawn in the pale sand upon which he lay. A strange painting, Laura thought, for Josie to have purchased — romantic, almost mystical.

Laura spent the next two hours searching the living room thoroughly. She looked beneath cushions, examined the cubby-holes and drawers in the roll-top desk, removed and studied every item in the twin bookcases. She shook every book, inspected every yellowed clipping, bookmarker, even a faded snapshot that fluttered to the floor. Again nothing, nothing at all unusual.

At about twelve-thirty, as she was in the process of exploring the kitchen pantry, she heard a knock at the back door.

Sheriff Tate politely removed his cap and held out a covered plate. "My wife's idea," he said, grinning awkwardly. "Better eat it before it gets cold." He followed Laura into the kitchen.

"Where's your lunch?" she asked.

"In here." He smiled, patting his stomach.

He accepted her offer of coffee and joined her at the heavy oak table as Laura ate with great pleasure the home-cooked meal — fried chicken, creamed corn, lima beans and warm buttered rolls.

"Your wife," she said, smiling, "is a marvelous cook! And it was very nice of her to do this. Thank her for me, please!"

"Yes, ma'am, I will." He shrugged. "She reckoned you ain't had the time yet to go shopping for ice and fresh meat and all." He pulled out his Salems.

Laura nodded. "I've spent all morning going through things in the bedroom and living room." She carried the empty plate to the sink and rinsed it off. "I was just starting in here when you arrived."

He looked at her with interest. "Anything missing, or different to you, so far?"

She shook her head. "So far everything looks normal to me — of course I've only covered the two rooms. But..." She paused. "There is one thing, though — that painting in Josie's bedroom. It wasn't there before. And there's something about it —" She broke off, frowning.

He followed her into the bedroom. Together they studied the painting. "It looks Victorian — at least the frame does," Laura said. "I can't make out the artist's name."

Tate rubbed his chin, peering thoughtfully at the painting. He pulled a small notebook from his jacket and scribbled in it.

They went to the living room. He lit a cigarette and paced the rug. Laura sat on the couch and watched him. Outside the sky was bright and clear, the ocean calm, deep blue, sparkling in the brilliant sunlight, the surf a distant murmur.

"Miz Westmoreland," Tate asked, "was your aunt a student of art, or an art collector?"

"Oh no," Laura answered. "She knew a little something about art, but no, I'd not call art one of her major interests."

"Then it's not very likely she bought that painting for its art value, or because it was a good financial investment?" He stopped pacing, looked at her.

She shook her head. "No. Actually, it's not even a particularly good painting. And it's rather, well — too romantic, I think, for her tastes." She frowned. "Maybe

she bought it for the frame. Or because it's Victorian."
She shrugged. "I really can't imagine exactly why she
bought it."

"Do you know what the painting is about?"

Laura hesitated. "I think . . . some story in Greek
mythology." She felt slightly embarrassed. "I'm afraid I
avoided the classics in college," she added with a weak
smile.

"Well, I'll check it out," said Tate. "I've got this
cousin, Pat. She's a schoolteacher, real smart woman,
reads a lot. Lives over on Roanoke Island, at Manteo." He
pulled out his small notebook, glanced at it. "I'll ask her
about this Cynthia and End — Endy, whatever."

Laura sat up suddenly. "Oh! Now I know what it is
that seemed — It's that circle in the sand! It reminded me
of —"

"Yes, ma'am!" he interrupted, nodding
enthusiastically, "that path of circles on the beach your
aunt drew a week ago. I thought of that too." He gazed
thoughtfully at the rug, then added, looking back at
Laura, "Something else mighty interesting too. The full
moon. It dominates the whole painting."

Laura's jaw slackened, her eyes widened slightly. She
stared at him, feeling suddenly chilled in the sun-filled
room.

His pale blue eyes were gentle, his voice sympathetic.
"This painting might be mighty important, ma'am," he
said. "It was, you know, exactly at the time of the full
moon that she drew those circles in the sand . . . and then
disappeared."

After he left, Laura thoroughly searched the
remaining rooms: the kitchen, bathroom, and The Closet
— not knowing what she was looking for, but dreading
the import of what Tate had said about the painting and

35

fearing she might find yet another sign of possible suicide. She was relieved that she found nothing else unusual inside the cottage. She found comfort in the sameness of these last three rooms, reassurance in the neatly-stacked worn towels and carefully arranged canned goods. Even The Closet had order in its seeming disorder, as it always had had. The drawers of the gray metal desk held neatly tied stacks of letters, all chronologically arranged.

Everything in the cottage reflected the Josie she had always known — organized, practical, sane, reserved. Everything except that painting in the bedroom. Laura re-examined it. Might it not be, after all, merely a period piece? Just another Victorian piece, like the Morris chair, the other furnishings? The moon, the circle in the sand — couldn't these be merely coincidental, unrelated to Josie's fate?

In the late afternoon, Laura put large pots of water to heat on the kerosene stove in the kitchen, then went for a walk on the solitary beach. In her sweater and white hooded jacket she was quite comfortable; the late afternoon sun minimized the chillness of the wind.

She tried to enjoy the seagulls and sandpipers, the rippled dunes and shell-strewn strand. She tried to forget about Josie for a while. But she could not avoid from time to time staring at the tranquil sea, imagining Josie's body beneath those seemingly harmless waves. Nor could she resist the urge to seek remains of the circles Josie had drawn. Finding none, she felt somewhat relieved.

At sunset she returned to the cottage. After a tepid bath by lantern light, she ate a light meal: canned tuna, crackers, and carrot sticks. After adding a log to the living room stove, she changed into flannel pajamas and a robe.

She adjusted the oil lamp beside the bed and flipped through the book on Josie's bedside table: *Ghost Stories and Legends of the Outer Banks.* Maybe reading about Blackbeard's ghost, she thought, would divert her mind from Josie. Book in hand, Laura pulled back the heavy quilt.

Then she saw it — a pastel blue envelope lying on top of the pillow. Neatly printed on the envelope: *LAURA.* In the upper left corner, the familiar dark blue monogram: *JWW.* She felt suddenly cold. She stared at the envelope, afraid to open it, praying it was not a suicide note, fearing it was.

Finally, trembling, she opened it. The neatly handwritten letter was dated: *Sunday morning, October 3, 1982:*

My dear Laura,

I deeply regret that you are, as you read this letter, probably *very* much upset. No doubt you fear by now that I am dead! I assure you I am *not* dead. Indeed I am in perfect health and in perfect happiness!

Beneath the house, under the kindling pile is a box buried just beneath the sand. The notebook inside it will explain everything to you regarding my absence.

I assure you, my dear, dear niece, that I am *perfectly* healthy, happy, and fulfilled. Do not grieve, for I am *not* dead!

With love to you *always,*
Josie

Astonished, Laura stared at this letter, then reread it. She felt confused and elated, puzzled and relieved, hopeful yet doubtful — but most of all, overwhelmed by curiosity. Quickly she grabbed the flashlight from the table drawer and went down the steep back stairs.

It took her half an hour to move aside the stack of kindling. A few inches beneath the exposed spot, lightly covered with sand, was a medium-sized, sturdy cardboard carton, sealed with postal tape. She quickly freed it from its bed of sand and took the carton into the cottage. She set it down carefully on the coffee table.

Her heart pounding, Laura poured herself a glass of Josie's white wine. Then she carefully knifed open the box. Inside, on top, was a pale blue looseleaf notebook with a typed label: *"My True Story.* By Josephine W. Westmoreland. For my niece, Laura W. Westmoreland. Completed on October 1, 1982."

Laura smiled at the absence of the middle name she and Josie shared, an old family name both of them disliked. She remembered the many times Josie had said to her, "Laura, when I'm dead and gone, if you let them put that name on my tombstone, I'll come back and haunt you forever!"

Beneath the notebook were half a dozen musty old books. Laura hardly glanced at these, so eager was she to read the *True Story* which would "explain everything" about Josie's sudden disappearance.

Paperclipped to the first page of the typed manuscript was another letter, also dated the third of October and apparently scribbled in haste:

Dearest L,

Have just reread, don't think I left out any important facts here, but must begin now the work on the beach. Did leave out (other note) one point. Forgot to mention I'm a homosexual, gay, lesbian, whatever your generation calls it.

Never got around to telling you before, probably should have, but you can't go back & change things. Not ashamed of it, just a fact, like my eyes are blue (yours too). We just didn't talk about it, my generation — jobs, families, etc., if not even jail! "Crime against nature" still in most states, especially South. We were mortally afraid to be honest!

Think I know you pretty well & it won't ruffle your feathers very much, but then Larry & Debbie, so conservative! Maybe shouldn't tell them? You decide. Won't matter to me, but consider their feelings, if would upset them, or you.

As for my *story* here, it's for you, & can keep it our secret if you like. Maybe easier to let Larry & others believe I *am* dead. Your decision, though.

Always my love to you,
Josie

Stunned, Laura reread this second letter. The third of October was probably the day of Josie's disappearance, six days ago. Laura wondered if "the work on the beach" meant those strange circles on the sand reportedly drawn by Josie.

But it was the part about Josie's homosexuality that had hit her, a revelation for which she had been totally unprepared. And yet this fact answered questions in the back of her mind for many years, such as why Josie had never mentioned romances with men. Laura reread the part reflecting Josie's attitude toward her homosexuality: "Not ashamed of it, just a fact, like my eyes are blue (yours too). We just didn't talk about it, my generation . . . We were mortally afraid to be honest!"

39

Avidly, Laura began reading the neatly typed manuscript:

This true story began in Richmond in September of 1954, when I was forty-two years old. I had been living alone for two years. Before that I had lived almost ten years with Marian, sharing our lives, and our bed, as married people do. You won't remember Marian. You were not yet five when she died: suddenly, of heart failure, August 5, 1952. A congenital defect, they said.

Since her death I had been deeply depressed and very much a recluse. I seldom even visited you and your parents. I suppose I could have sought a new love relationship, but I did not have the heart to do so, made no attempts at all to meet anybody. I just buried myself in my work at the Post Office. I lost all interest in love, relationships — life, almost. Then I had a dream that was the turning point in my life, although at the time I didn't realize it. This dream (as I later calculated) happened on the night of the full moon in September, a Friday night — or rather, early that Saturday morning. About a week later I wrote down this dream, which is why I can so faithfully record it for you here.

I was standing on a deserted hill (later I realized it was a dune) a short distance from a turbulent surf. It was very late, almost twilight, and I was alone. At my feet was a fish bucket, apparently mine. I saw something in it. At first I thought it was a large fish, but as I stooped to look, I saw it was a small black dog, apparently dead. I was startled it was there.

Suddenly someone was beside me, very close. A woman. In the vanishing light I could not see her clearly, yet I knew she was beautiful. I could not see this beauty, but I could *feel* it, vividly.

She said nothing, but smiled warmly and held out her arms to me. In silence I met her embrace. And instantly, I was filled with a passionate longing for her. We stood locked in an erotic embrace for several minutes, neither of us speaking.

Highly aroused, I pressed my body tightly against hers, knowing she shared my excitement. I felt an intense, climbing pulsation throughout my body. It felt like a wave — rushing, surging up and through and over me and then, in a climatic peak, breaking orgasmically and ebbing, throbbing gently. Even now I cannot write of this without again feeling, imagining that intense orgasmic surge.

Suddenly, the little dog I had thought was dead leaped from the fish pail and trotted away. This event broke our coupling embrace. Without speaking a word, the lovely woman took my hand and led me down the dune. Silently we followed the little dog and came to an isolated house on the beach.

We were inside the house. On a wall facing me was a large, very old oil painting, a portrait of a lovely woman. She resembled the woman I had just met, whose features, as I looked at her in the lamp light, were then distinctly, vividly clear to me — but not afterwards.

The woman in the portrait seemed to have lived centuries ago. Her face bore a sweet yet melancholy expression that stirred in me a mood of sadness, a depression I could not understand. For the first time in this dream, I spoke. 'Who was she?' I asked my companion. 'Was she one of your ancestors?'

In a soft, sad voice she replied, most strangely. 'Soon, once more I must be veiled.' Her tone was solemn, almost religious.

41

I sensed her puzzling words meant she was being compelled to leave me, being forced perhaps to join a religious order, to take the veil of celibacy. Pained, angered, frustrated at this thought, I asked her bitterly, 'Why? Why must you be veiled?'

She gazed thoughtfully at the portrait, then whispered, her back to me, 'It is the penance.'

'The penance for what?' I could barely conceal my pain at the thought of losing her.

Turning to me she replied solemnly, 'For mortal love.' Her large, dark eyes were filled with tears. I longed to take her into my arms again, but I could not move. Frustrated, bitter, I looked from her to the portrait and back again.

'Did she know mortal love?' I asked.

'No. Only immortal love,' she answered.

'But how can that be? For you are here,' I argued. 'She was your ancestor. She had to know mortal love.'

At this she smiled and shook her head as if I were a small child who could not understand her. Then she took my hands, drew me to her, and murmured lovingly, 'Do not be sad. Soon you will understand.' She stroked my face and kissed me tenderly. I was weak with desire for her.

'You must know mortal love,' I said, my voice breaking. 'You must love me!' I could hardly hold back my tears.

'I will,' she whispered. 'when I am next unveiled.' Again her body melted into mine. Again I was filled with intense emotion. But there was sorrow joined with ecstasy in this second erotic embrace. So that, this time, as that same rapturous wave swept up and over me, joy mingled with sadness at its cresting. And when I awoke, my eyes were filled with tears.

* * * * *

Stunned, Laura put down the notebook. This was a
Josie she had never known — a romantic, sensitive,
emotional woman with erotic fantasies, yearning for love.
Laura struggled to fit this image of Josie with her own
concept of her aunt as a reserved, business-like woman
who rarely displayed strong feelings. Fascinated, Laura
read on:

This was the most vivid, most realistic, yet also
certainly the strangest dream I had ever had. I was drawn
into it, and into the reliving of it, as if it had been an
actual experience. From that Saturday morning until late
that Sunday night, I moved about my house in a daze,
unable to accomplish anything except the most
mechanical tasks. Several times I lay down on the couch,
or on my bed, closed my eyes, and imagined again every
precise detail, feeling, and word that had been in that
dream.

I resented that Monday more than any Monday in my
entire life. Concentrating on my work took too much
effort. Several co-workers teased me about my
absent-mindedness, which embarrassed me greatly. I had
always been considered a model of efficiency.

Friday afternoon of that week, driving home from
work, I came terribly close to hitting a man on a bicycle.
Totally unaware of the traffic and biker, I had been in
another world entirely, the world of that fascinating
dream.

This near-disaster jolted me back to reality. I realized I
had become obsessed by a mere dream. I knew I had to
confront this dream and explain to myself both the

naturalness of it and my unnatural reaction to it, or I would not be able to function either at work or in society.

I spent the weekend rationally and systematically dealing with this obsessive dream. First, I wrote it down, detail by detail. All these twenty-eight years I have kept this detailed account of it. It was during the writing down that I realized I could not remember the woman's features, except that her eyes were very dark and bright and she was very beautiful.

Explaining to myself why I had ever had this strange dream at all was not very difficult. The dream had been, I concluded, an unconscious, final confrontation with my loss of Marian. It had expressed my deep, undying love for her, my inability to accept the loss of her, and my irrational hope to be reunited with her in another life, another realm. How relieved I was once I had analyzed this obsessive dream so efficiently as this! Now I could forget it.

Another realization that weekend was that I badly needed a change of scenery, a long vacation. It had been unwise to absorb myself in my work. I needed to get away from Richmond, from the scene of Marian's death.

On Monday, I requested three weeks off as soon as possible. Since I had taken no time off for two years, my supervisor immediately granted my request.

Marian and I had several times vacationed on the Outer Banks in the early fall, at Nags Head. I knew the surf-fishing was excellent there this time of year and that there were many miles of solitary beach I would enjoy. So when a co-worker offered to rent me his three-room beach house on Hatteras Island for the first three weeks of October, I was delighted.

Hatteras was even more remote than Nags Head in those days; the inlet bridge had not yet been built. I remember how pleased I was that only two other cars were waiting for the ferry the afternoon of my arrival.

The tiny cottage I had rented was ideal, comfortable but simple: bath, bedroom, combination kitchen and parlor. Wood-paneled inside, wood-shingled outside, with a modest porch facing the ocean. There was electricity and running water and a radio if I wanted it (television had not yet reached the Banks) — which I did not, any more than I wanted a telephone (and none was there). I had a good supply of books to fill the evenings and the rainy days. The rest of my waking hours I meant to spend outdoors, walking and sometimes surf-fishing.

And of course I had with me my journal, to record impressions, thoughts, feelings. I had always kept such a daily journal, a fact about which I would later be most glad. This habit has enabled me to keep accurate track of important dates in my life, and to ensure accurate memories.

I moved into this small cottage on October 8th of 1954. For the first four days I simply enjoyed the scenery, the restfulness, and the exceptionally pleasant weather. I fished, took long walks on the isolated beach, read, wrote in my journal, and slept better than I had for the past two years. I thought of Marian often, yes — but more often now with joy than with sadness, remembering the happiness of loving her more than the pain of losing her.

I began to feel at peace within myself, to enjoy again a happiness in the simple pleasures of life I had not felt since Marian's sudden death. And then, on the fifth evening of that week, occurred the event that changed my life forever.

The afternoon of October 12th had been perfect — cloudless, calm, brisk, yet not too cold. I had wandered much farther north along the beach than I ever had

45

before. As sunset neared, I realized I had no idea how far north I was from my rented house, how long it might take me to walk back.

On an impulse, I climbed the dunes, thinking perhaps from there to get my bearings. But all I saw south was the sameness of this barrier island landscape: sea and shore, dunes and low-growing bushes. The nearest cottage southward was beyond my vision.

The sun was setting now, and I had to be at least an hour's walk from my cottage, but I did not care. I wanted to linger on the dunes, to enjoy the brilliant sunset. I looked toward Pamlico Sound. A narrow desert lay between me and that serene inland sea, a sea-formed desert broken only by scattered patches of squatty, wind-bent shrubs. Beyond this deserted expanse, like a wide golden-red ribbon, lay the waters whose western shore I could not see. The sole sign of human life on the sandy stretch of island was the deserted two-lane highway running north and south, a dark gray intruder down the yellow-gray sand.

The dropping sun transformed the sound gradually into a band of shifting colors: fiery red, softer orange, then dusky rose and deep lavender. I imagined myself some explorer of old, the first person ever to watch this natural splendor.

I looked then at the Atlantic. The panorama there was also exhilarating. Along its horizon, the virtually cloudless sky was a tapestry of muted dark pastels: deep rose, lavender, dark purple, and every shade of blue I had ever seen. And all these heavenly hues were mirrored in the waters, but with spangles of darkness and light caused by the ceaseless motions of the sea.

Directly before me, in the multi-colored sky I saw the rising moon — peach-pale and glowing softly. A full moon, reflecting the warm light of the lingering sunset. To me it seemed the most beautiful rising moon I had ever seen.

Twilight was drawing near. I wanted to stay there forever on the dune, but knew I needed to start homeward. I began making my way down through the deep sand toward the smooth beach.

Halfway down I happened to look seaward, and something caught my eye, a movement, a shape — something just beyond the breakers. Something alive perhaps, I thought, or maybe some piece of wreckage, surfacing after decades, even centuries, from one of the countless ships destroyed along this dangerous coastline.

Curious, I descended the dunes quickly and ran to the surf's edge. The object kept disappearing from my view behind the mounting and breaking waves. Then it bobbed upward momentarily, riding an incoming swell, and I saw by its splashing that it was something alive and apparently swimming, or struggling to swim.

I stepped to the very edge of the surf. Lifted by another swell, the creature came closer, now only about twenty yards from me. I saw then it was not some sea animal playing in the surf, but a small, dark dog, trying desperately to reach the shore.

In the obscure half-light of twilight and moonrise, I stood transfixed by the sight of that tiny animal battling that enormous, darkening gray sea, a relentless, uncaring force that would swallow this tiny being. I yelled, 'No!' and shouted to the dog, 'You can make it! Don't give up!' But even as I shouted, it disappeared beneath a foaming breaker.

'Don't die!' I shouted, as if by sheer will I could rescue this animal. I saw its head again. Impulsively I threw off my jacket and sneakers and waded into the icy water. Instantly I was filled with fear! For as you know, Laura, I

47

cannot swim. The little dog's chances for survival were better than mine if I waded too deeply into that surf.

A breaking wave crashed hard into my thighs, almost knocking me off balance. The undertow pulled violently at my feet and legs. Freezing and frightened, I started to turn back. But I saw the little dog again, only a few yards from me now, an almost human look of sheer panic on its face. I could not let it drown. Battling the seaward sucking of the surf, cautiously feeling for my footing, I edged closer to it. A wall of churning foam slammed against my stomach. I struggled to keep my balance, the current tugging fiercely at my legs. Bone-cold, more frightened now, again I started to turn back to shore.

Then the dog resurfaced only a few feet to my right. I saw the terror in its eyes and knew I could not abandon it to the sea. Carefully I edged toward it, shaking with cold and fear. A head-high breaker crashed violently into my chest and face, sucking me beneath the blackening water. I thrashed wildly for footing, for air, for survival! I struggled to my feet, gasping, and waded as fast as I could back to shore.

In knee-deep water I paused, looked around for the dog, hoping it too had made it ashore. I was trembling violently from the cold water, the wind, and my near-brush with death.

Suddenly, something beneath the dark water bumped against my leg. I jumped with fear. Then I saw what it was: the little dog I had meant to rescue. Before the surf could suck it seaward again, I grabbed it. The dog was limp, motionless, apparently dead. Yet I hugged it to my chest and ran up onto the beach.

Shivering uncontrollably, clutching the dog tightly, I grabbed my jacket and shoes and climbed up the dunes to gain protection from the wind. I collapsed in a hollow behind a dune and struggled into my sneakers and jacket. Then for some minutes I just sat there in the sand, hugging the lifeless little dog, wishing it were not dead, feeling grateful that I was not. I continued to hug the limp animal for the scant heat it offered. I had never been so cold in my entire life.

Suddenly I heard a woman's voice, shouting words indistinct to me. Her voice came nearer. Then I saw her, standing at the crest of the dunes. She called out words I did not recognize. Then she ran swiftly down toward me. In a moment she was on her knees reaching out to me — or rather, to the lifeless little dog.

Miraculously, at her touch the small black dog I had assumed was dead struggled to free herself from my arms. Amazed, I released her. Wagging her tail happily, she rushed into this woman's arms as if that near-drowning had never happened.

Twilight had deepened into early night. I could not clearly see the features of this woman. But the full moon was unusually bright, so I could see her well enough to know she was younger than I, perhaps thirty, and also quite beautiful. She moved gracefully, in an almost stately manner.

Her long hair, worn in an upswept fashion, seemed the same color as the moon that shone upon it. She wore a long, pale yellow gown, almost like a nightgown. And over this, a cloak of a deeper hue of pale yellow, fastened below her neck by a glittering golden chain. Her pale slender feet were bare. Her attire seemed odd for this season and this setting.

For several moments there was a silence between us. Still shivering from my plunge into the icy Atlantic, I sat hugging my knees to my chest, trying to warm myself. And she, seemingly scarcely aware of me, sat nearby,

49

cradling the dog against her breast, rocking it gently and murmuring as if it were her child. I felt suddenly envious of that dog, then almost angry that compared with her dog's ordeal, my own near-brush with death seemed insignificant to her.

As if she had read my thoughts, the lovely woman suddenly released the dog, removed her cloak, and placed it gently around my shoulders. Then she stood smiling radiantly down at me, seeming more beautiful than before. Her eyes, large and dark, black like a moonless night, seemed flecked with starry lights.

No longer did I feel the cold. No longer did I feel the clammy wetness of my sea-soaked clothes. I felt now only a sudden, inexplicable longing for this radiant woman. I struggled to my feet, fighting this longing, and I made a weak attempt at normal conversation. 'How . . . how is your dog?' I asked.

She simply nodded toward the animal, which lay a few yards away complacently grooming herself with a casualness I found startling.

I gazed again at this mysterious woman. In an apparent outburst of gratitude, she pulled me to her and hugged me warmly. I felt excited by this embrace and wanted to prolong it, yet I was fearful of doing so. After a moment I pulled away, stammering that there was no need for her to thank me, asserting that the dog had really saved herself.

The stranger's response was simply a glowing smile. Then she took my hand, led me up the dune, and pointed to the beach below. There, only a dark spot on the smooth strand, was the little dog, trotting northward in the bright moonlight.

'Come,' said the lovely woman. 'She is leading our way.'

Staring at this tiny figure in the distance, I suddenly felt a strangeness I did not understand — perhaps shock, fatigue from my plunge into the water and frightening near-drowning.

'Come,' the woman repeated. 'You are wet and cold. Come now with me. Soon will you be dry and warm.'

Not waiting for a reply, she led me quickly to the beach. And like an obedient child, I walked silently hand-in-hand with her north along the sand, in the direction the little dog had taken.

We came to a small beachfront cottage, wood-shingled and dull gray in the moonlight. It looked old, virtually abandoned. We climbed the steep wooden steps up the low dune to the planked porch. We entered the cottage. Silently, swiftly, my hostess lit a quaint old lantern and suspended it from a hook in a beam above the couch. Then she drew back the curtains from the twin windows facing the sea. The room was bathed in bright moonlight.

She stood a moment with her back to me, gazing at the moon. Then she broke our long silence. 'Come,' she said softly, turning to me, 'you must undress and bathe away the salt.' She lit two tall, creamy-white candles and handed one to me. Then she led me to a bathroom whose fixtures seemed very old. She turned on the taps in the heavy, claw-footed tub. Flowing hot water steamed in the chill air of the room.

'All you require is here,' she said, nodding toward an ornate dressing stool which held towels and a thick white robe. She lit more tall pale candles and placed these on a low round marble table at the foot of the tub, twin to the small table at the tub's head, which held now the two candles by whose light we had entered. On this first marble table also was a delicately carved crystal vial.

From it she poured into my bath water a few drops of a perfume of exotic aroma.

'Bathe now,' she said, smiling, 'and I will prepare our meal.'

Before I could even thank her she left. I settled happily into the hot, inviting water. The dim candlelight, the hazy steam, and the exotic scent filling the small room combined to create an almost hypnotic effect. I relaxed utterly. My mind slammed shut like a finished book, and I yielded myself wholly to the pleasures of my senses. I thought of absolutely nothing. Yet I felt absolutely everything. And with no conscious effort, I recorded every minute detail of this time and this place, all I felt and saw etched forever in my memory, from the spherical shape of the yellow soap to the flickering of the creamy candles.

Like conscious thought, time too seemed suspended. I do not know how long I stayed in the bath. But I remember the candles were very low when I wrapped myself in the warm white robe and left.

Laura stopped, puzzled. She reread this description of the stranger's bathroom with its claw-footed tub and marble tables. Then she reread the descriptions of the outside of the mysterious woman's cottage, and of the living room — the lantern, the couch, the windows. She was startled, concerned. The house Josie was describing seemed not a stranger's house, but her own — this very cottage Laura was sitting in. Yet it had not existed in 1954. Josie had designed it, supervised the building of it, and finally moved into it in 1960.

Somewhat shaken, Laura poured herself a second glass of wine and read on:

* * * * *

Just beyond the entryway to the living room I paused, spellbound, and stared silently at my hostess, whose back was to me. She was on her knees before the fireplace, resting on her heels, her head bent toward the flames, tending a fire she had built. It and the bright moon were all that illuminated the room — except for one tall pale candle on a small round wooden table between the beachfront windows. This candle glowed just beneath the moon, which had climbed further upward into the star-studded sky above the sea.

I watched, motionless, as she unpinned her upswept hair and shook it lightly, spreading it with her fingers. Her moon-pale hair fell full and free down below her shoulders, gleaming brightly in the glow of firelight and moonlight. What happened at this instant I could not understand. Suddenly I found myself experiencing what seemed a waking dream, a brief hallucination.

I felt myself — no, I *saw* my self, or my soul — leave myself, my body rather, and walk quietly up to her. I saw my *self* drop to my knees behind her and then bury my face in that mass of moon-pale hair. I drank in the exotic perfume of it, the same scent as that perfume in my bath. And I felt my self stroking her silky hair, softly sweeping it back from her neck, and then with gentle passion placing my mouth delicately against her smooth, warm neck. And I felt my tongue softly tracing the contours of her neck and my hands delicately exploring her waist and breasts as I encircled her and pulled her body gently backward into mine.

No sooner did this happen, or seem to happen, than instantly I was again inside my body, standing in that exact same spot near the entryway! I felt faint. I gripped

53

one edge of the entryway, my eyes still fixed on her. I was breathing heavily. My legs felt weak, my mind confused.

Meanwhile the lovely stranger, still kneeling before the fire, tilted her head slightly backward, then down toward her left shoulder. And with her right hand, she swept back her hair, baring her neck precisely as I had thought or dreamed I had done just that moment before. And, hugging herself tightly, she made a soft, low sound — barely audible. The unmistakable sound of deep pleasure, as if a lover were kissing her on her neck.

I felt then as if I were losing contact with reality! My head was swimming, my legs almost collapsing beneath me. I grabbed the arm of the couch tightly and struggled to maintain consciousness. The woman stood, her back still to me, and said softly, 'You must have some wine now.'

I collapsed onto the couch just as she turned to face me. Thankful the lighting was dim, struggling to calm myself, I murmured, 'Yes, thank you.' I prayed my voice sounded normal.

She smiled and walked toward me, holding a glass of white wine. 'Did the bath restore you?' she asked, offering the glass.

I hesitated. 'Yes . . . I think so. But now I feel —' I broke off, rubbing my forehead, and reached out thankfully for the wine.

'It was your trial,' she said gently. 'The freezing waters. Your fear of drowning. The wine will restore you, and food, and the warmth of the fire.' She smiled and took my hand. At this touch I felt strangely revitalized. I also felt relaxed, at peace again, as I had felt moments before in the bath.

She draped an afghan across my lap and tucked it around my legs. 'Soon you will feel much better,' she said, her dark eyes glowing brightly. 'Rest here. I will return with food.'

I felt relaxed, contented, warmed by the afghan, the fire, the wine. She was right, I thought. It was my trial, as she had so quaintly called it, that had caused this strange hallucination minutes before. If I had not gone into that surf to rescue her dog, then —

Suddenly it struck me: Where was the dog? I had risked my life for this animal. Where was it now? Just at that instant, the lovely woman reappeared, carrying a large round silver tray holding dishes of food. She set this tray on the marble-topped table before the couch and smiled at me warmly.

I asked about the little dog. She looked deeply into my eyes. 'Have no fear,' she said. 'She is safe. She is in her element.'

I glanced around the room. 'She's here? In your house?'

'No.' She shook her head. 'Not in this place. But she is safe always, in her own element.'

I was puzzled by her words. 'Where is that?' I asked. It struck me then that English was not the native language of my hostess, nor America her native land. This explained the strangeness of her speech and clothing.

'Not yet may I explain,' she replied. 'But always she is safe. Do not trouble your mind. Do not think of her more.'

My mind was troubled, however. But she began serving our food, and the sight and smell of it distracted me. Every dish was intoxicatingly exotic. There were pieces of fruit bathed in spices I could not identify, vegetables in sauces alien to me, small morsels of meats I did not know, marinated in sauces I could not recognize. I assumed these were dishes from her native land. I ate with the greatest pleasure, almost as if I had never truly enjoyed food until then.

Our meal was strangely silent, yet also exciting — almost sensual. Our eyes met often and I saw that she took pleasure in my pleasure in the food. A few times I asked about her native land, but she seemed reticent, reluctant to answer me, so I did not press her.

I was uneasy still about the whereabouts of the little dog that had almost cost me my life. Toward the end of our meal I raised this topic again. My hostess, refreshing my wine, replied, 'Fear not. Believe in me. Her task has been fulfilled, and she is safe.'

I drank my wine, too quickly. It struck me then, to my astonishment, that we had not even exchanged names. 'What is your name?' I asked somewhat thickly.

'Selene,' she answered with a smile.

'See — what?' I realized then I was almost intoxicated.

'Se-*lee*-ne,' she said.

'Selene,' I said. 'That's a lovely name!'

'By some I am called Cynthia, but I am Selene. Still other names have I been called,' she added.

'Like what?' I asked, rubbing my forehead. I felt somewhat dizzy.

'There is one name,' she said, sighing, 'that is not true! It is not I!' She added bitterly, 'This name I hate!'

'Is it your middle name?' I asked, giggling slightly. 'I hate my middle name too!' I grinned sheepishly.

She smiled at me, shaking her head. 'You do not understand,' she said softly. She rose and began clearing the table.

I leaned back on the couch, watching her. 'What do you want me to call you?' I asked.

'I am Selene, Josephine,' she answered, walking away swiftly with the silver tray of dishes.

'When did I tell you —' I stopped, realizing she was no longer in the room. I could not remember telling her my name. I rose to go after her, but found I was unsteady on my feet. I dropped limply back onto the couch, cursing myself for gulping the wine.

When Selene reappeared I asked her for a cup of coffee. She looked at me blankly and repeated, 'Coffee?' I remembered she was from a distant land. 'Yes, coffee,' I explained. '*Café*. It's like tea, somewhat, but black. And stronger.' She looked at me, puzzled still. 'The wine, you see,' I explained. 'I'm afraid it has gone to my head.' I felt suddenly as if I might lose consciousness. I bent over and put my head between my knees, praying I would not get sick.

Selene moved quickly to my side, sitting by me on the couch and putting her arms gently around my shoulders. At this embrace I felt myself tense, for her close presence excited me.

'Have no fear,' she whispered, as if she had read my thoughts. Her scent was all about me, that exotic perfume of my bath water. I relaxed. Gently she pulled me back into her arms, repeating, 'Have no fear.' Her face brushed my cheek. I longed to turn and kiss her, but I was too weak to move.

'I am here,' she murmured lovingly. 'And I am at the full. Have no fear, my beloved. Believe in me. I am here to love you.'

So intoxicated was I by the wine, by her strange words, and by her perfume and the sensation of her body against mine, that I could not speak at all. I was very close to unconsciousness, yet also delightfully awake and relaxed, filled with serenity, peacefully happy. I was aware that my conscious being was slowly shutting in on itself, as one closes a book slowly. And yet at the same time, my senses seemed unusually alert. All that I heard, saw, felt — all of it was extraordinarily vivid to me.

I remember how Selene rose quietly, gracefully from the couch and looked down lovingly at me. I remember how she gently placed pillows beneath my head and draped the soft afghan across me, tending me like a careful mother. And I remember too the silence, broken only by the muffled booming of the distant breakers.

She stood motionless at my side for some time, her head bowed as if in prayer or meditation, her back to the oceanfront windows. Bright moonlight bathed her head and shoulders. The full moon framed her head like a halo. And just as I was slipping into sleep, Selene's self seemed to melt into and become as one with that radiant moon.

I awoke in a strange bedroom. It was still night. The moon shone brightly through a long, tall window thinly veiled with sheer curtains, and I could see my surroundings. On an antique bedside table a tall pale candle burned brightly. I was lying in a large old bed, a four-postered bed, beneath a thick, warm quilt.

My mind was completely clear, my senses keenly alert. I felt warm, comfortable, thoroughly relaxed, yet also revitalized and intensely alive. Strangely enough, I did not at all question where I was or why.

I sat up in the bed. Facing me was a heavy antique bureau. I could see myself dimly in the oval mirror above it. I saw I was nude above my waist. Slipping my hands beneath the quilt, I found I was nude entirely. I caressed my body languidly for a moment and felt vaguely aroused.

Suddenly, the door into the room opened quietly. And standing before me in the doorway was Selene. She wore a long, flowing robe seeming to be of that same almost transparent fabric which curtained the window. I gazed at her speechless, drinking in the loveliness of her as she stood there motionless, smiling at me. Her long pale hair and her body glowed in the moonlight streaming through the tall window. Her large dark eyes glittered above the flickering flame of the creamy-white candle she held.

I was overwhelmed by her beauty. I stared at her open-mouthed, amazed, enchanted. Days later I would remember a poem by Lord Byron that captured my response to this sight of Selene in the doorway:

> She walks in beauty, like the night
> Of cloudless climes and starry skies;
> And all that's best of dark and bright
> Meet in her aspect and her eyes:
> Thus mellowed to that tender light
> which heaven to gaudy day denies.

I remember fearing this moment was only a dream, or a marvelous vision. I remember digging my nails into my bare thighs, feeling the pain from this assault upon my flesh, and knowing from this pain that I was very much awake, and she was most definitely before me.

I started to speak, if only to say her name. But Selene, moving gracefully toward me, placed two fingers to her lips and slowly shook her head. So in silence I held out my arms to her.

She placed her candle beside the other one on the bedside table. In silence she unfastened her sheer robe and dropped it to her feet. She bent toward me in her nude splendor. Trembling, I wrapped my arms around her slender waist and buried my face in her smooth, warm breasts, my eyes wit with tears of joy.

In a moment she was with me in the bed, covering my mouth, my throat, my cheeks, my shoulders with kisses such as I had never known — not even with Marian. Kisses such as I had never imagined could be.

I cannot describe to you the absolute ecstasy of our love-union that night — not because it would embarrass me to describe it, no, but because my words are unequal to the task. But I will try to relate to you some sense of the perfect joy we shared — the beauty, the tenderness, the fulfillment of it.

All sexual and emotional pleasures possible between two women in love were shared between us that night, yet magnified beyond my wildest dreams. I grow weak even as I write this, remembering those many hours of absolute bliss.

It was as if — what? As if we were both eighteen, even younger, and were love's novices, overwhelmed with delight at our first discovery of love. I remember trembling with awe and excitement each time I touched any part of Selene. It was as if never before had I put my lips to a woman's breast, never before entered a moist, welcoming vagina. And each time Selene touched me, it was as if I had never been touched before. Each orgasm was as if it were the first, or the most fulfilling, I had ever known. And yet each surpassed the one that had come before it.

Yet it was also as if we had been loving each other forever. I did not need to ask what things would please her. I knew. And all that I did delighted her. And Selene knew also what my own desires were, and fulfilled these beyond my deepest fantasies. As the night deepened, our love-making intensified beyond all dreams. It was as if together we were climbing an invisible ladder of love and passion that soared into infinity. Often we wept, trembled, sobbed with ecstasy. Often I felt my soul had left my body, felt I was dwelling in some fantastic paradise.

I remember the candles consumed themselves long before our lovemaking ended. I remember the pre-dawn sky beginning to eclipse the moon and stars. And I remember Selene's words to me as I lay against her warm body, totally spent and completely fulfilled, my arm draped limply across her smooth abdomen, my face buried in her moon-pale hair and warm neck. I was falling asleep. She whispered softly, almost sadly, 'Now I must leave you, my beloved. But I will return to you, at twilight.'

At the edge of unconsciousness, I made a feeble gesture to stop her from leaving my side. But she kissed my eyelids softly, and instantly I fell into a deep and dreamless sleep.

Never in the six months since Laura had stopped smoking had she longed so much for a cigarette. Josie's night of lovemaking with a beautiful woman from a foreign land — had it actually happened? It seemed so real to Josie. And yet the bedroom described — it was Josie's bedroom surely. In this cottage, which did not exist in 1954.

Laura reread the account of the lovemaking. She found herself strangely moved — even somewhat aroused. She thought of Jackie. This was what Jackie had wanted with her.

They had been sitting side by side on the couch in Laura's apartment.

"I more than love you," Jackie said, taking Laura's hand. "I'm in love with you, Laura . . ."

Laura remembered again the loving look in those dark brown eyes. Remembered too pulling back her hand, looking away, saying coolly, "I'm sorry. Apparently you've misunderstood . . . I can't —" She stood, quickly walked away from Jackie, hugging her arms tightly and trembling inside.

Jackie followed her, faced her, gently taking Laura's shoulders. "Can't we talk about it?" she pleaded.

Laura tensed, averted her gaze.

"For God's sake, Laura!" Jackie's voice broke. "Look at me!" She gripped Laura's shoulders, her hands trembling. "This is me, Jackie, remember? I'm not some monster because I love you." She released Laura's shoulders and looked away, tears streaming.

Oh how Laura wanted then to hug her, to . . . But a buried fear shut down all her emotions. She looked at this wonderful, handsome woman, her dearest friend, with an almost icy detachment. "I'm sorry," she repeated, turning away from Jackie. "But I cannot —" Folding her arms tightly, shaking inside, she had added, her back to Jackie, "I think . . . I think it would be best if, if we stopped seeing each other . . ."

Never would she forget that stunned, incredulous look on Jackie's face. Never would Laura forget the sound of the door slamming.

Laura sighed, running a hand through her hair, wondering again at her incredible cruelty, her cold rejection of friendship as well as the offer of love. How many times had she lifted, then replaced, the telephone receiver, wanting to apologize to Jackie for that savage wound, but not knowing how to explain herself?

She tried to push aside the memory of that strong, tanned face, those brown eyes, the thick black curls that trailed down Jackie's neck. The three years of happiness they had shared.

Laura fixed black coffee and checked the time. It was after eleven. She returned to Josie's manuscript:

When I awoke, I was alone. Bright sunlight filled the room. It was shortly after noon. I got up and wrapped myself in the thick bathrobe, which smelled faintly still of that exotic scent I would now associate forever with Selene.

The cottage was cold, silent, empty. The fireplace had been swept clean of its ashes. In the glare of daylight, the living room's furnishings appeared very old, very dusty — even disused.

I went to the bathroom. The toilet flushed, but did not refill afterwards, and when I turned to wash my hands at the sink, there was no water. I was amazed!

Shivering, I went into the kitchen, which I had not yet seen. Like the rest of the house, its furnishings were antique — an old kerosene stove, grey with dust; a round oak table, also dusty; an ancient wooden ice box, absolutely empty. Empty too were the pantry shelves and the cabinets beneath the water-stained old sink. I was astonished to find nothing here to indicate this kitchen had been used the night before — not a scrap of garbage, not a salt shaker, not a single match.

I was somewhat relieved, however, when I noticed the small china cabinet in the corner, for in it I saw the dishes and wine glasses from the evening before. Yet when I tried the tap at the sink, hoping for a glass of water, I was again amazed! Not one drop of water. I dropped the glass, which shattered in the basin.

Shaken, almost doubting my senses, I went into the living room and stood for a while before the cold fireplace. Had I wandered alone to this deserted cottage, disoriented after my icy plunge in the ocean? Had I simply dreamed all the rest — Selene, the bath, the glowing fire, the meal and wine, the lovemaking? I shook my head firmly. No, I had not dreamed these events, I knew. Selene and our night of love had indeed been real. Yet where was Selene now? I asked myself uneasily.

I wrapped myself in an afghan against the chill and sat down on the old couch. Methodically I recalled everything, from my attempt to rescue the dog onward. I remembered Selene's words, her gestures, her clothing, her body. I remembered our lovemaking. I tried to recall the exact words she had whispered to me at early dawn, as she left my side: 'Once more I must be veiled, but I will return to you at twilight.'

Suddenly I realized that 'Once more I must be veiled' had been the words of the woman in my dream the month before.

And suddenly, Selene's face and the face of the woman in my dream blended in my memory and became one face!

And I was gripped by fear — fear of myself, fear of my own imagination! Was I losing contact with reality?

Frightened by this possibility, I hugged my knees tightly. The white robe slipped aside. I saw on my thighs the nail marks I had inflicted upon myself the night before, when Selene had first entered the bedroom. I was enormously relieved! These scratches were real, this white robe was real — Selene's robe, not mine. I was as certain that Selene had brought me to this cottage as I was certain that it existed.

I returned to the bedroom. My clothes, clean and dry, neatly folded, lay atop the antique bureau. Slacks, sweater, jacket — everything was there. I dressed quickly in the uncomfortably cold room.

Still I felt compelled to reassure myself that I had not dreamed the events of the night before. Like a detective I closely examined the bed. I found some pubic hairs on the sheets. Elated, I grabbed the pillow next to mine, Selene's pillow, and pressed it against my face, inhaling deeply. Yes, it was her perfume. Overjoyed, laughing, I fell across the bed, hugging her pillow, kissing it lovingly.

Rolling onto my back, I cupped my hands over my mouth and nose and inhaled the musky scent still lingering on my fingers — Selene's scent, not my own. No, I had not wandered alone to this strange cottage and merely dreamed of love. I had made love to the beautiful Selene.

I made the bed, then left the cottage. The beach was deserted as far as I could see, north and south. I welcomed this isolation. In the crisp, sunny autumn air, with no companions except an occasional gull which kept its distance, I walked for some time back and forth along the strand near Selene's cottage, happily absorbed in my own thoughts and feelings.

I concluded that there was no mystery in Selene's absence. She had said she must leave but would be back by twilight. No doubt she had just last evening arrived at the cottage and had brought with her only the provisions for one meal. Now she was away at some nearby village, shopping for food and other provisions she would need while staying at this cottage, such as ice and firewood.

No doubt there were additional errands that would fill her day. I remembered the waterless faucets. The plumbing was old; something must have broken overnight. No doubt finding a plumber was one item on Selene's list of errands.

Pacing the beach and thinking things through like this, I soon decided I had simply allowed my over-active imagination to suggest a mystery where there was none. Selene herself, I thought to myself with a smile, was most definitely as real as I.

Quite hungry now, I walked quickly south along the strand for a long time, finally reaching my own rented cottage. I ate a salad and a sandwich, took a shower and changed my clothes. Then I stretched out on the couch and thought of Selene. Without meaning to, I fell asleep.

I dreamed I was on the beach, and it was extremely dark. There was no moon, no stars. Only by the dusky-dim foam of the in-washing waves could I distinguish the sand from the water. Everything seaward was one immense, horizonless stretch of blackness.

I heard Selene's voice, calling to me. But I could not see her. I could not even be certain of the direction of her voice. Then her voice seemed nearer to me, close to the water's edge. I stepped toward her voice. An icy wave washed across my feet and I drew back, frightened.

Then I heard Selene's voice again — distant, almost indistinct. 'Do not fear,' she called. 'I will return to you.'

'Where are you?' I shouted into the blackness all about me, filled with fear of this darkness and of the crashing waves. Yet filled also with a painful longing to find her, touch her again.

Her voice came again from the blackness, barely audible, drowned by the roaring waves and wind. Only two words were clear to me: 'Veiled' and 'penance.' I groped about blindly in the blackness, shouting out 'Selene! Selene!'

Suddenly, a cold, skeletal hand seized my shoulder. And a low, hoarse female voice hissed at my ear: '*Hecate!*' I jumped violently and tried to scream.

Still struggling to unlock the scream from my throat, I awoke, breathing in heavy gasps. For minutes I still felt that icy hand imprisoning me and heard echoing in my ears that strange word, '*Hecate!*'

The room was dim. Knowing it would soon be twilight, I pushed this nightmare from my mind. All I could think of now was Selene's promise to be with me again. There was not time enough to walk to her cottage. Angry at myself for having fallen asleep, I grabbed my car keys and rushed out of my cottage.

Twilight was rapidly approaching. No sooner did I get into my Ford than I realized I had made two very foolish mistakes in addition to falling asleep. I had returned from Selene's cottage to my own by the beach rather than the road, and, before leaving her house, I had failed to look at the back of it, the side facing the road. I had no landmarks to go by in looking for it, nor did I know how many miles from my own cottage it was. The increasing darkness and the sameness of the island's landscape would further handicap my search.

I took some comfort in the sparse population of the area; beachfront houses along this stretch were few and widely separated. Yet there was that sameness to them, as to the land, that would complicate my search. Virtually every house had the same rectangular shape, the same exterior of grayish, weathered wooden shingles. And not all of the houses were visible from the road.

I passed some cottages that were dark, shuttered, closed down until spring by their mainland owners. These I ignored, concentrating on the houses with lighted windows, that had cars or trucks parked in the drives. I drove north, then south, then north again along a ten-mile stretch north of my rented cottage. As twilight deepened into nightfall I cursed myself for not knowing what kind of transportation Selene had.

I began now to stop at the occupied houses, to knock at the doors, only to be disappointed by the faces that answered. I described Selene to these strangers, but none of them knew her.

It was quite dark now. Lost, angry at myself, very frustrated, I parked my Ford in the oyster-shelled drive behind the next old cottage I came to, which was dark, apparently unoccupied. I climbed up the dunes and down to the beach. I marked this spot where I was with a large piece of driftwood. Then I ran and walked, ran and walked, north of there along the beach for several miles. The few houses I came to were dark or, if lighted, did not have the twin windows or the porch of Selene's cottage.

Disappointed, weary, fearful I would never find the house, I ran and walked south until I reached my driftwood marker. There I sat to rest for a moment, meaning to search in this same way southward. I was exhausted, depressed — and most of all anxious, fearing Selene might believe I had forsaken her. I felt foolish too, almost guilty. I longed to find her, to explain what had happened, to have her forgive my stupid errors and hold me in her arms again.

As I thought of her I stared blankly at the sea and sky. The night was clear and cloudless, as before. The moon hung full in front of me, just above the horizon, making a pathway of silver across the undulating ocean, a dancing, sparkling path from the horizon almost to my feet. I stared at this silver path that floated on the swells as they dipped and rose and crested.

Suddenly I felt very calm, peaceful, inwardly serene. My conscious mind seemed to close in on itself. All thought vanished; all fear and frustration vanished. I felt then one thing only, a deep inward sense of completeness and love. I saw then only the moon and its undulating, sparkling path across the water.

I closed my eyes and dropped my head into my hands. And I envisioned Selene, haloed by the moon. I remembered her face, her long pale hair, her dark bright eyes, her voice, her touch. A deep longing swept over me like a cresting wave. I yearned for her. I ached for her.

Then suddenly, above the murmuring of the surf, I heard a woman's clear, soft voice: 'I am here.'

And there before me, glowing in the moonlight, stood Selene — at the very edge of the wet sand, the very edge of the moon's silver path. I was speechless, overwhelmed with happiness, yet suddenly too weak to move from my driftwood seat. I watched spellbound as she walked quickly to me across the smooth, firm sand.

She knelt before me and took my hands in hers. She pulled me gently to my feet and embraced me warmly. 'You have found me,' she said softly. 'Come, my beloved.' And then, like a bewildered lost child found by her mother, I walked in blissful silence beside her, hand in hand, to the cottage just behind us — the cottage where I had parked my car, the cottage I had thought was deserted.

All things within the house were as they had been the evening before. A cheerful fire warmed the room, its rich aroma mingling pleasantly with the exotic scent of Selene's perfume. In the glow of firelight and moonlight, the furnishings seemed brighter, newer than they had appeared to me that morning.

On the small, richly polished round table between the windows, two golden candlesticks rested. In both of these Selene immediately placed creamy white tall candles, and lit them. As she turned to face me, I saw that they stood left and right of the full moon hanging above the sea, like bright attendant stars.

As before, Selene placed food and wine on the marble table before the blue couch and, as before, we ate almost in silence. Questions, like ghosts, floated through my mind, but I dared not voice these, for as I looked at her, so radiantly beautiful, again I feared I was in some deep, exotic dream. If so I wanted to do nothing to awaken myself from it.

After our meal, we lay together on a braided oval rug before the fireplace. And with her delicate, smooth fingers, Selene traced the outline of my face. I pulled her hands to my mouth and gently kissed her palms and fingers. I felt safe now, yet filled with an overwhelming need to share with her my strange dreams and my fears.

I told her first about the dream that had so obsessed me the month before, concluding that it seemed now to have been a prophecy. She smiled and kissed my forehead. 'Yes, beloved Josephine,' she murmured, 'this dream was true.'

I told her then about the nightmare I had had that afternoon. She listened solemnly, staring sadly into my eyes as I described my terror of the darkness and of losing her, and my horror at the ice-cold touch of the bony hand upon my shoulder and the sound of the evil female voice in the blackness. She looked pained, and turned her face from me briefly when I said the word *'Hecate.'* Her shoulders quivered slightly in the brilliant moonlight.

She arose and stood gazing quietly at the moon for a moment. Then she lay again by my side and hugged me tightly. 'Have no fear,' she said reassuringly. 'This dream was false. I will have you always. Hecate will not take you.'

'I don't understand this nightmare,' I confessed. 'I'm afraid of it! It too was so real! What if it too becomes true?'

She sat up, leaning back on her heels, and looked deeply into my eyes. Her dark eyes glittered brightly in the glare of the firelight. Firmly, gravely, she said, 'Disbelieve this nightmare. This second dream is false. It is not real.'

I sat up on my elbows and gazed into her eyes. 'Is *this* real?' I asked, frightened by my own question. 'This moment? This place?' I felt my throat tighten, my head grow light.

She stopped my questions with a long deep kiss. Then, releasing my lips, but holding my shoulders firmly, she again stared deeply into my eyes with those dark, radiant eyes that seemed to have the power to penetrate my very soul. I met her gaze as if I were an infant.

'You know that this is real,' she said solemnly. 'Am I not real?' She took my hands and placed them over her warm breasts. Through her thin, silky gown I felt the hardness of her nipples against my palms.

'Yes,' I said, 'you are real. This moment is real . . . But what is Hecate? That cold, evil —'

'Listen to me, me only,' she interrupted. 'Listen not to your secret fears. Disbelieve this false dream.'

I stared intently into her eyes, absorbing her every word. Her eyes grew even more brilliant as she spoke. She held my hands tightly.

'Hecate is not real,' she said earnestly. 'You must disbelieve in Hecate. She is but a myth, but a name for all that you fear. A name for the unseen darkness.' She paused and tenderly kissed each of my eyes.

'Soon will these eyes be open more,' she continued. 'But now, like the infant, you fear the darkness still. You

71

will learn from me to disbelieve in Hecate. Then she will vanish.'

She arose and looked down at me lovingly. I gazed up at her spellbound, not understanding her words and yet believing them. Her yellow hair and gown glowed in the moonlight. I drank in the sight of her loveliness, a beauty beyond all description.

'Believe in me,' she said softly. 'Then Hecate cannot touch you. She is the dark. I am the light. She is the false. I am the true. Believe in me, my beloved.' She smiled and took my hands, pulling me gently to my feet.

I felt strengthened by her touch, filled with vibrant life. 'Yes,' I said firmly, 'I will believe in you. I will disbelieve in Hecate.' Not yet did I know the meaning of this promise. Not yet did I understand Selene's mysterious words. But I knew beyond all doubt that Selene was as real as I, and that this moment was true.

We spoke then no more of my dreams or fears, but only of our love. There before the glowing fire, Selene made love to me — not simply to my body, but to every fiber of my being. As she kissed my forehead, my eyes, my mouth, she sealed her soul into my soul. Her lips against my throat, my shoulders, my breasts, pulled my heart into her own. Her body pressed upon mine became one body, ours. And when her soft hair brushed across my abdomen, and her warm breath spread across my flesh below my navel, and her smooth, delicate hands gently parted my inner thighs, I felt my entire being melting into hers.

Laura sighed and stared at the night sky. This love Josie was describing — she had to have known something like it, sometime. With some woman. Perhaps with Marian, if not this ethereal Selene.

Laura had felt the reality of this love, this passion, even as she had been reading Josie's words. Had felt somehow that she understood what Josie meant about the tenderness, the beauty, the completeness of such love.

She thought again of Jackie. In Jackie's eyes she had seen the offer of such love, had heard it in Jackie's voice, felt it in her gentle touch . . . had fled from it, saying "I cannot."

Why couldn't she forget that painful final scene? Why would it not stop haunting her? Laura shook the image of Jackie's pain-filled eyes from her memory and concentrated again on Josie's story:

When I awoke that second day, October 14th, I was again alone in Selene's cottage. It was a gloomy, overcast day. In this dull gray light the house seemed almost oppressive in its silent emptiness. It seemed again musty, abandoned. I had no memory this time of Selene's leaving me, but knew she would return to me here once more at twilight.

I dressed quickly. Out of some irrational fear, I did not enter either the bathroom or the kitchen, but swiftly left the house. The deserted beach looked bleak; the surf was unusually rough. Still, I felt warm and happy. I recorded my odometer reading before I started my car, determined not to get lost this coming evening when I returned.

Back at my own cottage, I spent this rainy afternoon writing down every detail of the events of the past two nights. My detailed journals from that day onward have enabled me, Laura, to give you this faithful account these twenty-eight years later.

After writing, I took a long hot bath and dressed. By now it was raining quite heavily and the wind was very strong. My watch told me it was well before sunset, but the storm-darkened sky told me there would be no visible distinction between sunset and nightfall. Anxious to again be with my beloved Selene, I put on my waterproof parka and ran quickly through the driving rain to my car.

The rain and wind intensified as I drove the deserted road. I could barely see twenty feet ahead of me, even with the headlights on. But I knew the precise distance to Selene's cottage because of my odometer reading that morning. I was confident I would not get lost again.

Still, when I arrived at the cottage, I feared I was indeed lost, for no vehicle was parked there. Nor could I see any light at the back windows. I could barely see the features of the cottage itself through the deepening darkness and heavy rain.

I ran quickly through the ankle-deep rainwater to the steep wooden steps leading to the back door. I was soaked before I reached the door. The narrow overhanging roof offered little protection from the wind-driven rain. I pounded hard on the door. There was no answer.

The door was unlocked, however, so I entered the cottage and loudly called out Selene's name, slamming the door behind me to shut out the wind and rain. There was no reply. I called again. Still there was no response. It was so dark inside I could barely see two paces before me. I moved forward cautiously, still calling out, 'Selene? Are you here?'

As I neared the living room, my eyes adjusting to the dark, I dimly saw the beachfront windows. Somewhat relieved, certain now I was in the right cottage, I located a lantern and lit it. Then I saw the familiar couch, fireplace, roll-top desk, bookcases. Everything was as before, except that Selene was not there.

I pulled off my rain-soaked parka and soggy tennis shoes. Shivering in my soaked socks and semi-soaked jeans, I quickly built a fire, all the while wondering where Selene was. I felt increasingly uneasy, imagining she must be journeying toward the cottage in this blinding rain as I had just done.

Thinking about this second day-long absence from her cottage, I remembered that not everyone on this island in mid-October was here on vacation, as I was. Perhaps, I thought, comforting myself that Selene's daytime absences were not mysterious, perhaps she worked in one of the villages, or was seeking employment in one of them.

Standing with my back to the fire, drying and warming myself, I noticed on the coffee table the decanter of white wine and two wine glasses. I poured myself a glass, then returned to the warmth of the fireplace. As the minutes ticked away, however, I became increasingly anxious about Selene. The wind and rain had intensified; the windows were rattling noisily. I wondered if I should get into my car and search for her. But how could I? I did not even know what kind of car she had — if indeed she even had one.

Feeling considerably uneasy at the thought of how very little I actually knew about Selene, I quickly finished my wine and walked toward the coffee table to put down my empty glass. Even before I reached the table I felt suddenly light-headed. Wondering how one glass of wine could have this sudden effect, I sank onto the couch. The room began to swim before my eyes. Startled, I stretched out on the couch and closed my eyes, fighting this inexplicable feeling of intoxication.

I do not know how long I lay there with my eyes closed. During this interval my mind closed in on itself. Perhaps I slept, or dozed, or fell into some reverie. I do remember that while I was in this strange state of suspended consciousness, the image of Selene dominated my senses. I imagined seeing her, feeling her presence, smelling her exotic perfume. I felt her arms about me and heard her voice lovingly speaking my name.

Suddenly I revived from this state. I opened my eyes and saw Selene standing at the foot of the couch, smiling at me. I shook my head, only half-believing my senses. 'Selene?' I questioned, rubbing my eyes, 'is that you? Are you here?'

'Yes, my beloved,' she answered softly. 'I am here now.'

'Thank goodness!' I exclaimed, sitting up quickly. 'I've been worried! This storm. I was afraid —'

She stopped me with a warm embrace and a kiss on my forehead. 'Have no fear,' she said reassuringly. 'I am always safe. These elements do not touch me.'

'You're braver than I,' I said with a little laugh. 'I hate driving in such weather. But when did you arrive? I must have been asleep.'

'I came as before, at twilight,' she said.

I noticed that my watch had stopped running. Pulling it from my wrist to reset it, I asked what time it was. She shrugged and shook her head. 'I do not know time as you speak of it,' she said.

'You mean you don't have a watch?' I asked. 'A timepiece like this?' I held out my watch. 'Or a clock?'

'No.' She smiled. 'I know only that this is the time of our loving.' She pulled me gently to my feet and kissed me. Then she lifted the decanter and started to pour wine for us both. I stopped her hand. 'None for me, my darling,' I said. 'Not at present.'

She looked at me surprised. 'My wine does not please you?'

'Your wine pleases me very much! But you see, I had a glass earlier.' I grinned sheepishly. 'I guess I drank it too fast.'

'Do you wish then water at present?'

'Yes, that would be fine. Or coffee —' I stopped, remembering that coffee seemed alien to her. 'Water,' I added. 'Water's fine.'

She looked deeply into my eyes and frowned slightly. 'You speak not the truth,' she said. 'Be never afraid to speak to me truly of what you desire. Whatever you desire I will provide when I am here. You desire coffee, yes?'

I shrugged. 'Well, yes, but —'

'Then I will create it for you. Wait here, beloved.' She kissed my forehead lightly, and quickly left the room.

I sank into the couch, relieved and happy she was there with me again. I was utterly enchanted by her voice, her gestures, her quaint use of the English language. I thought it delightful she had said she would 'create' coffee for me.

She returned soon with a steaming cup of delicious coffee, the best I had ever tasted. I thanked her with a kiss. Then she moved to the oceanfront windows and lit three tall pale candles on the round table between them. It was then I realized that the weather had changed dramatically. The sky was filled now with bright stars, and the moon, still full, hung brightly halfway up the windows.

'This is amazing!' I exclaimed. 'I must have slept for a very long time! When did the storm blow over?'

'When I arrive,' she said, walking toward me, 'the elements are once more calm.' She kissed my brow and left me again, returning soon with the silver tray holding our meal.

77

As she knelt before the table, spooning the food onto our plates, I noticed again the three candles burning at the windows. The night before, Selene had placed two candles there, and the first night, only one. 'Those candles,' I asked, nodding at them, 'are you counting by these the evenings of our love?'

'Yes.' She smiled, unpinning her upswept hair, which dropped in graceful pale waves beneath her shoulders. 'Also,' she added, 'these signify more.'

'What?' I asked curiously.

'In time I will explain,' she answered. 'But now, let us dine.'

The foods we ate were, as before, unknown to me, exotic — yet delicious beyond description. The strangeness of this meal prompted me to question her again about her native land. I asked where she had been born.

She answered, 'I was incarnated first in this world on the mount called Cynthus.'

'Where is that?' I asked.

'On the island called Delos, in the sea called the Aegean.'

'Oh!' I said brightly. 'Then you are Greek?'

She smiled and shook her head. 'No. The Greeks claim me, but so also do the Romans.'

'Half Greek and half Italian?' I asked, laughing lightly.

Again she shook her head, then took my hands and looked deeply into my eyes. 'I am of all places, yet none,' she said solemnly. 'It is not permitted yet to say more. Believe I will love you now and forever, beloved Josephine, and question no more.' Her large black eyes glittered brightly. She raised two fingers to her lips and slowly shook her head.

We finished our meal in silence. I no longer felt a need to know where she was from or why she was there with me. I cared only that I would love her, and she would love me, forever. After the meal, she whispered, 'The waning has begun, beloved. Come quickly now.' She took my hand and led me to the bedroom. And as before, on this, our third night together, we loved each other with a rapture beyond my powers of description, our bodies bathed by the radiant moon and soft candlelight.

CHAPTER THREE
Midnight, October 9

Laura rose from the couch and gazed absently at the star-studded sky. The moon appeared briefly from behind a thin cloud, then vanished again, as if winking at her. It was a half-moon.

She walked somewhat wearily to the kitchen. As she stood before the kerosene stove refreshing her coffee, she was keenly conscious of the station wagon, silent and empty, beneath her feet, under the cottage.

She sighed and walked back to the living room. Picking up Josie's manuscript again, Laura stared thoughtfully at the title page: *My True Story.* She shook her head sadly and read on:

Early the next morning, October 15th, I was roughly awakened by fierce weather. The wind was howling, whining mournfully through the heavy rain and rattling the windowpanes. I rolled toward Selene. But as before, she was not there.

I got up quickly. The view from the bedroom window was startling. Never had I seen such ugly weather. The rain gusted in wind-driven sheets. The surf crashed violently, the waves breaking high up on the beach as if it was high tide — not due yet for many hours.

I dressed quickly and went onto the beachfront porch, thinking I should lower the storm shutters. I couldn't reach the latches, however, and could barely stand in the fierce wind; and even with my parka I was quickly drenched to the skin. I retreated to the house, fetched a kitchen chair, and returned to the porch. Finally I secured the front shutters.

Back inside the cottage, I debated whether to try to shutter the back windows. I decided not to, remembering that my own cottage was probably now in more danger, sitting closer to the sea. I locked the two doors of Selene's cottage and left.

The road was so flooded that in some places I feared my car might stall, the rain so heavy that the windshield wipers were virtually useless. I inched along in first gear. All the while I was frantic about Selene, having no earthly idea where she was. All I could do was pray she was safe. I cursed myself for not knowing where she spent her days.

When I finally reached my cottage, I was amazed. The surf was breaking only a few dozen yards from it. Almost in a state of panic, I struggled with the storm shutters on the ocean side. Grape-sized pieces of hail began to beat down with the rain, and a windowpane near me shattered violently.

Just then I heard a man shouting. I looked toward the road and saw him racing toward me, his army raingear flapping wildly. As he ran up the steps to my porch, he yelled, 'Hey, lady! What in the hell are you doing here?'

I stared at him blankly. The brawny, olive-skinned young man rushed onto the porch. 'Come on!' he shouted above the wind. 'We gotta get outta here! Right now, lady!'

'What — What is it?' I stammered.

'Jesus Christ, lady, don't you know?' He stared at me in disbelief. '*Hazel,* that's what!'

'Hazel?' I looked at him puzzled.

'*Hazel!*' he repeated excitedly. 'A hurricane, lady! Ain't you been listening to the radio?'

'No,' I answered, feeling both foolish and very frightened.

'Lucky we spotted you! Our truck is gonna be the last vehicle off the island — if we make it.' He pointed toward an army truck parked on the flooded road. 'Come on! Let's go!' he yelled.

'What about my car — my clothes?'

'Hell, lady,' he shouted above the wind, 'forget 'em! Your car won't make it to the ferry — if there's still a ferry when we get there. Let's go! Right now! *Go get in the truck!*'

I darted past him into the cottage and he followed, shouting angrily, 'My God, lady, you ain't got time to pack! *Forget* your clothes! Forget *everything!* The road's washing out already!'

I grabbed my pocketbook and my journal and ran with him to the truck, hugging these two things to my chest.

'You sit up front,' he ordered, 'with the driver.' He climbed into the canvas-covered back of the truck.

I climbed into the seat beside the blond young driver, whose uniform identified him as a private in the Army National Guard. As we drove away I asked him about the hurricane.

'Hazel's the worst one in a lotta years, ma'am,' he said, peering through the streaming windshield. 'She's done wiped out the South Ca'lina beaches — nothing much left from Myrtle Beach on up to Wilmington. Looks like she's gonna do the same thing to the Outer Banks,' he added grimly.

'Listen,' I said anxiously, 'I have a friend here! We'll pass right by her house. We have to stop there! We *must!* She doesn't know! She doesn't have a radio,' I explained frantically.

He nodded. 'You show me her place,' he said. 'We'll check.'

Never before had I concentrated so carefully on locating Selene's cottage. It seemed like hours before we reached it. Finally the driver brought the truck to a grinding halt in her driveway. In army raingear he raced up the back stairs, while the other soldier ran up the dunes to the front of the house. In moments the other man reappeared, waving his arms and yelling something I couldn't hear to the young driver, who was pounding on the back door. Both men ran quickly back to the truck, water streaming from their raingear.

'Nobody there!' shouted the driver, yanking open his door. He jumped into his seat and threw the truck into gear.

I felt the blood leaving my face. 'Are you sure?' I asked, grabbing his arm.

'Positive! Front door's open. Fred went inside.'

'I locked it!' I exclaimed. 'With the deadbolt!'

'Hazel's unlocked it, ma'am,' he replied solemnly, backing out of the driveway.

I seized his arm again. 'Wait!' I said frantically. 'She'll be back! I know she will! Just leave me here,' I pleaded.

He stared at me amazed. 'Lady, you crazy? In a few more hours there ain't gonna *be* no cottage here!' He backed onto the highway and shifted gears. The truck lurched forward through the deep rainwater flooding the asphalt.

I stared numbly at the streaming windshield and began to cry softly.

'Look, ma'am, I'm sorry,' he said gently. 'Didn't mean to upset you. But there's nobody in that cottage. No vehicle there either,' he added, his tone brightening. 'So you see, she must of got off the island already! I'm sure she's safe.'

Selene's words came back to me then: 'I am always safe. These elements do not touch me.' A strange calmness swept suddenly over me. I closed my eyes and visualized Selene. For a long time I sat in silence, hearing in my mind her reassuring words: 'Have no fear. I am always safe. These elements do not touch me.'

Laura remembered hearing her parents and Josie talk about Hurricane Hazel when she was a child. Josie had been rescued from the hurricane by National Guard soldiers. This much of Josie's story had to be true. But the mysterious, and missing Selene? Laura read on:

The truck rumbled and swayed as we eased along the dock, up the ramp, and onto the ferry, which held several other army vehicles. The young blond driver and I sat silently, tensely, in our seats inside the truck, feeling the boat beneath us wallow and vibrate with shudders as the engines shoved us away from the dock and into the heaving, churning waters of Oregon Inlet.

I glanced at my young blond companion. Was it rainwater on his forehead and upper lip? I looked with fright at the foaming water pouring over the deck, closed my eyes and prayed silently. The ferry boat rose and fell, rose and fell in the huge swells, wallowing also from side to side. I fought against nausea, gripping the dashboard to steady my swaying body. I was absolutely terrified.

I heard above the wind and rain a loud thumping and pinging. I opened my eyes. Golfballs of hail pounded and danced on the ferry's metal deck and the hood and roof of our truck. Suddenly a fierce gust of wind snapped a wiper blade from the windshield and hurled it into the water. I jumped violently and looked again at the driver. He was gripping the vibrating steering wheel with white-knuckled hands and licking his lips nervously.

'Dear God,' I said aloud, 'don't let us drown!'

'Amen!' he said, swallowing hard.

So relieved were we when we reached the ferry landing that the young driver and I both whooped with joy. As we were docking, he released the steering wheel, hugged me spontaneously, laughed and lit a cigarette. He offered me one — and I almost took it! As he eased the truck down the dock and onto the flooded highway, he said, 'Well, ma'am, I reckon the worst part's over.'

'Where are we going now?' I asked.

'Roanoke Island. They're using the school at Manteo as a shelter.'

'Then we'll have to cross Roanoke Sound,' I said somewhat anxiously, thinking of the narrow old bridge.

'No sweat!' he said confidently. 'After that boat ride, the bridge'll be a piece of cake.'

He was right. The bridge ran due west, so that the wind was at our back, no longer slamming at the truck sideways. When we reached the inland island, we picked up speed. 'Boy, look at them pine trees!' my companion said happily. 'See how they're cutting the wind?'

'Yes,' I said, nodding. 'But still . . . it's an island.'

'Oh but you'll be safe here,' he said reassuringly. 'A good six or seven miles back from the ocean. And if they decide it ain't safe, they'll evacuate you to the mainland, across the Croatan Sound bridge to Mann's Harbor, you know.' He paused, then added, 'It's gonna be okay now, ma'am. No need for you to worry.'

Selene's words came back to me again: 'Have no fear. I am always safe. These elements do not touch me.' I felt these words applied now to me, as well as to her. I sat silently thinking of her.

'Probably find your friend here, ma'am,' said the driver.

'What?' I was startled that he too was then thinking of Selene.

'Your lady friend, back on Hatteras. She's probably here at the school,' he explained. 'If she ain't, you just check with the Red Cross people, see if she's at another shelter.'

Selene wasn't on Roanoke Island — not then, not ever. Those two-and-a-half days I spent at the shelter in Manteo were a nightmare. I wandered through a crowd of countless strangers — refugees from the Banks, Red Cross workers, local volunteers. I described Selene to hundreds of people. None had ever seen her; none had ever heard of a woman named Selene. I moved numbly for hours through the hallways, the cafeteria, the gymnasium, searching for her face in the sea of strangers crowded into the school. Often I was on the brink of despair, but at such times I held fast to the memory of her words: 'Have no fear. I am always safe.'

I kept my sanity through sheer effort. I still had my journal. I spent hours rereading it, finding peace in my memories of that idyllic time before Hazel. I also spent hours recording what I saw and felt while at the shelter. I forced myself to eat, and I tried to sleep, but all I could manage was an occasional doze on my army cot in room 10, the classroom-turned-dormitory I shared with two dozen women and children.

All of us stood in line for everything: meals, showers, clean used clothing. I stood in line to use the toilet. And I remember standing in line for almost three hours that first evening, waiting my turn to make a three-minute telephone call to your parents, Laura, to let them know I was safe. Your mother cried hysterically when she first heard my voice. I can't remember what words we said.

Crying was universal at this place. People wept openly at news of the dead and injured. They wept at reports that their homes were gone, their cars, their boats, their businesses. The older children sometimes joked and laughed nervously, hiding their hurts and fears behind grown-up expressions. The uncomprehending younger ones wept frightened tears because their parents wept.

On the morning of October 17th came the shocking news: every oceanfront house on Hatteras Island had been totally destroyed. The army driver's grim prophesy rang in my memory: 'There ain't gonna *be* no cottage, lady.'

I wandered about the gymnasium in a daze, bumping into people, my eyes blinded by tears. Then I ran down the hall to room 10, sobbing uncontrollably, and collapsed onto my cot.

Some time later I remember Selene had not been in the cottage. That it was gone did not mean she was dead. 'Have no fear. I am always safe,' I whispered to myself repeatedly. And deep within my soul grew the conviction that I would soon return to Hatteras, soon find Selene there again, untouched by this disaster.

Your father found me late that afternoon. He had driven down from Richmond as soon as the weather and roads had permitted. I collapsed in his arms — actually fainted from relief and joy at the sight of his face in that sea of strangers: the face of someone I loved, my dear brother, your dear father.

Exhausted in body and spirit, I fell asleep almost as soon as we got into his car. I think I slept all the way to Richmond. And after we reached your home, I went almost immediately to bed. I slept in your bedroom, Laura. You were just a little girl then. Maybe you will remember the twin beds you had.

Laura smiled, remembering the matching beds, painted white and decorated with decals of rabbits and flowers. She dimly remembered awakening with surprise one morning to find Aunt Josie asleep in her other bed. She read on:

That night, sleeping in your room, I had a dream in which Selene appeared to me. She stood, a shadowy figure, at the window beside the bed where I slept. Her features were dim, her voice but a whisper. She called my name.

'Where are you?' I asked her. 'I can hardly see you.'

'Fear not. I am safe,' she said. 'Now begins the veiling time. But I will be with you again, at the full.'

I strained to hear her words. 'I don't understand!' I said with frustration, yearning to see her, hear her, more clearly.

'Remember the moon,' she said, her voice a fading whisper. 'Come again to the place of the house that was, when next the moon is full. There I will come to you. But speak of me hereafter to no mortal, lest I vanish from you forever.'

I remember reaching out toward her shadowy form and pleading, 'Don't leave me!' But at that moment she vanished into blackness. I awoke suddenly and stared at the window where she had stood in my dream. High in the sky I saw the moon, small and dim now, approaching its last quarter.

Remembering Selene's warning that I would lose her if I spoke of her to anyone, I never told your parents any of these facts I am writing to you here. From that night onward I dared tell no one of her existence.

Getting a week off from the Post Office in November was simple. I had used only one of my three weeks of vacation time before Hazel struck, and my supervisor was quite sympathetic to my request to return to Hatteras as soon as possible to document my losses for insurance purposes. He in fact urged me to take as long as I needed.

At the Currituck Sound bridge I was stopped by two armed Army National Guardsmen, one of whom asked for my identification. I handed him my driver's license. He flipped through papers on a clipboard and shook his head. 'I'm sorry, ma'am,' he said. 'You're not listed here. Nobody's allowed in but residents and property owners.' With his adolescent voice and pimpled face he looked like a Boy Scout. I felt like shaking him!

'But I was here, during Hazel!' I exclaimed. 'You have to let me in! I had to leave my clothes behind, my car!'

'I'm sorry, ma'am, but you're not listed here,' he replied, shaking his head and looking again at the clipboard. 'Not a resident —'

'Listen! I was renting a cottage, on Hatteras Island! I was evacuated. I had to leave my things, my car! You *have* to let me in,' I insisted.

He looked from me to the used Chevrolet I was in. 'I might believe you, ma'am — that you lost your car, but —'

He was interrupted by the honk of a jeep arriving from the Outer Banks end of the bridge. There were three Army Guardsmen in it. Parking the jeep about ten feet away, the driver grinned and yelled, 'Shift's over, boys!' As he walked toward us, I recognized the voice, the lanky frame, then the blond hair and youthful face. I jumped out of my car with excitement. '*He* knows I was here!' I said with joy. 'He's the one who rescued me!'

A smile of recognition spread over the face of my former companion. 'Well, I'll be,' he said with a grin. 'The last lady! How about that! How you doing now, ma'am?'

90

I laughed with relief. 'Fine!' I said. 'Except this young man here won't let me in. I suppose he thinks I'm a looter!'

'She's not on the list, sir,' the guard stiffly explained.

'She's sure on mine,' the driver replied with a grin. 'Your shift's over, private. You two fellas go on over to the jeep.' He took over the clipboard and waved for the relief guards to stay back for a minute. As we stood alone he winked at me and said, 'Give me your name again.' He wrote it down on the list, filled out a card, and handed it to me. He grinned and pointed to his shoulder. 'Corporal now, ma'am. Because of Hazel. And you.'

I congratulated him, thanked him for rescuing me yet again, and drove on. You probably remember the old Currituck Sound bridge, Laura. So narrow that two cars could barely meet and pass. Trucks were always scraping gray paint off those thin metal rails. I marveled that all three miles of it had made it through the hurricane.

About a mile beyond the bridge another soldier stopped me to explain about the detour down the Banks. 'The paved road's gone, ma'am,' he said, peering at me through horn-rimmed glasses. 'Broken up, most of it. Washed out. How far you going?'

'Hatteras Island, the north end.' I said.

He shook his head. 'Gonna take you quite a while, ma'am. Speed limit's fifteen. It ain't much of a road now.'

I was very glad I had left Richmond at dawn. The temporary road laid down by the army engineers was designed for World War II battlefields — and the sturdy tires of trucks and jeeps. Mile after mile of long narrow sheets of webbed metal hooked end to end across the sand. With the worn tires on my used Chevrolet, I dared drive no faster than ten miles per hour. It was like driving on a washboard.

It took me almost two hours just to reach the inlet. For about the first hour I could hardly believe the hurricane had ever happened, so undisturbed, so serene was the landscape. Gulls glided along the coast on gentle currents, white wings against the cloudless blue sky. The deep blue sea seemed sleeping, so calm it was. And all about me endless miles of undulating land — dunes bright white in the afternoon sunlight with shadowed valleys of yellow-brown sand. Flat sandy fields of wind-swept grasses sweeping west toward the sound and the dark stunted pines.

But as I crept past the tiny village of Kitty Hawk I was stunned by the devastation that broke this serenity. Heaps of rubble that had been homes. Houses sagging seaward, leaning precariously, ready to collapse at the slightest breeze. Broken concrete blocks, boards, shingles — scattered about like confetti. A battered truck perched on a roof half-buried in the sand. Snapped telephone poles, twisted waterlines protruding from empty foundations, buildings with one wall, like Hollywood sets. Bizarre sights, horrifying — a boat in the hollow of a huge dune, half a mile back from the ocean; a baby's crib by the roadside, a dead cat in it.

It was as if dozens of bombs had blasted this little village. I silently prayed for the dead and wounded.

But there was life here too. People picking through the debris, salvaging what they could of their homes and businesses. Army trucks, pickup trucks carting away mounds of rubble. Guardsmen everywhere, directing traffic, checking identifications, assisting with the clean-up efforts. Army tents, a Red Cross station, a bakery truck delivering free bread. I felt heartened by these sights. The Bankers would rebuild, I thought — would survive, even thrive. They always had, since early colonial times.

One manmade monument remained untouched — the Wright Brothers Memorial, looming to the west south of Kitty Hawk, towering as always atop the high grass-covered hill, dwarfing the low landscape all about it. I felt renewed respect for the mid-western brothers who had come to this remote and precarious place to initiate the age of aviation. Rekindled respect too for the Bankers who had assisted them, helped provide the food and shelter, the water and firewood that had enabled them to survive those fall and winter months of 1903.

That same ironic contrast I'd seen at Kitty Hawk, and then at Kill Devil Hill, met me once more at Nags Head. To the east, devastation; to the west, tranquility. That great mountain of sand, Jockey's Ridge, visible for miles before I reached it, soared skyward still above the gently rolling landscape — as solid a landmark as it had been for centuries.

Finally I reached that long, uninhabited stretch between Nags Head and Oregon Inlet. It too was the same narrow desert of sand dunes and sea grasses it had always been. An occasional gull soared peacefully overhead in the clear blue sky.

Close to the inlet I saw the decaying carcass of a large dog, with macabre grin and fly-infested sockets. I looked away, sickened and saddened. Then I felt enormously thankful my own life had been spared, and Selene's also. I brightened at the thought that I would be with her again quite soon.

The inlet waters were placid in the late afternoon sun. Here and there, lapped by tranquil ripples, stood pilings, the few remnants of the ferry boat dock. This sight chilled me. How soon after our army truck had driven down that dock, I wondered, had it crumbled into the inlet?

The metal washboard road led me to a nearby spot where army amphibious craft were moving people and vehicles to and from Hatteras Island. During the crossing of myself and my car I sat quietly, grimly remembering my narrow escape across this inlet the month before.

It was almost twilight when I reached Relief Station Three on the island. This small tent town, operated by the National Guard, brought back unhappy memories of my evacuation to the school in Manteo during Hazel. Drab army green canvas dominated the landscape; crude wooden signs were everywhere. I parked in the webbed metal lot and walked across the sand to the tent marked Registration.

As at Manteo, I was processed, except now I filled out forms asking for everything except my sexual preference. The stocky sergeant behind the table handed me a pamphlet, Civilian Regulations and Procedures, and a map, Hatteras Island: Relief Station Three. On the back of my identification card the red-faced heavy officer scrawled 3-F. Happy at the thought I would soon be with Selene, I attempted a small joke. 'I see I'm 3-F,' I said with a smile, 'not 4-F. Am I in the army now?'

He did not even smile. 'Tent Three, to the right,' he said blankly, waving me away. 'Follow the map, please.' I nodded and left quickly. Night was falling.

Tent Three was large, and labeled Single Female Civilians. It was partitioned into semi-private sections with canvas walls and lettered door flaps. My 'room' was F. It contained an army cot, two wool blankets, a pillow, a hand mirror, a kerosene lamp, and a small kerosene heater. A wooden platform served as the floor. I smiled, thinking again of Selene as I lit the lantern in my drab quarters.

It would be useless to begin my search for the ruins of Selene's cottage before daylight. In the deepening darkness I joined the line outside the mess tent. After a bland dinner of canned beef stew, canned string beans, loaf bread and coffee, I returned to my quarters, lit the kerosene heater, wrapped myself in a wool blanket and wrote down the day's events in my journal. Exhausted from the day's driving, I then went to bed. But I was so happy and excited at the idea of being with Selene again that it was several hours before I fell asleep.

Selene came to me again. I could see her vividly! The scent of her enchanting perfume was all about me. I felt her touching me, lovingly caressing me and kissing my body. I sighed and reached out to her.

'Yes, I am here, my beloved,' she whispered. I felt her mouth and her body melt into mine. And afterwards she murmured, 'Tomorrow you will find the site of our earthly home. There you must recreate the cottage. It must be as it was before.'

She left my side and stood before me, a radiant form against the darkness. 'Do not leave me now, beloved,' I pleaded. I tried to reach out to her, but my body would not move. She bent to me, her pale hair brushing my face, and touched my eyes, closing them gently. 'Now must I leave you,' she whispered, 'but I will come to you again at twilight, at the site of our earthly home that was and that shall be again.' All was blackness when I opened my eyes.

As Selene had predicted, that morning I found the remains of our house. I knew the spot instantly by the claw-footed bathtub on its side, half-buried in the sand. In the rubble I recognized also the blue couch, the kerosene stove, pieces of the bed, other items. I was overjoyed at the sight of each relic, broken or whole.

My search was interrupted by a freckle-faced soldier who asked for my identification. I produced my card, explaining I was not the property owner but had visited a friend in that cottage just before Hazel and was to meet her there soon. As I was talking two men approached us, a white-haired elderly man with a cane and a dark-haired man about my own age.

'The old gent coming yonder's the owner,' the soldier said. He then moved on.

I got up my courage to introduce myself, for I realized that to rebuild the cottage, I would have to convince the elderly man to sell me the ruined property, using whatever tactics my goal might demand.

Mr. Willoughby, the owner, was a southern gentleman of the old school, a native of Raleigh, he said with pride. He was thin and stoop-shouldered and wore a three-piece wool suit and a bow tie. I lied, telling him I had been born in Durham.

'That so?' he asked with interest, his watery blue eyes brightening.

'Oh yes,' I said, adding with a sigh, 'but then my family had to move — to Richmond, when I was a little girl.'

He digressed on the topic of the Battle of Richmond for a while, then introduced the man with him as his son-in-law, whose last name I can't recall, although I know it was an Italian name. 'Al here married my baby girl, my only child,' Mr. Willoughby said. 'Took her and the grand-young'uns off to Florida a few years back.' He glanced at the son-in-law with a slight frown. 'Didn't leave me and her mama much choice after a while but to move down there too — if we wanted to see her and the young'uns.' I quickly realized Mr. Willoughby did not much like either Florida or the son-in-law.

'Leaving Raleigh must have been hard for you,' I said.

'Yes indeed,' he said, shaking his head sadly. 'So you were a Tar Heel born?' he asked, changing the subject.

I smiled. 'Yes, sir! And a Tar Heel bred, too!'

He beamed. 'Your folks were natives, then?'

'Oh yes!' I lied. 'Tar Heels all the way back, for five generations.'

'Any of 'em in the War?' he asked.

I knew which war without having to ask. I named the first Civil War battle in North Carolina that popped into my head. 'Fort Fisher,' I said. 'The battle over Wilmington. One of my ancestors died there.' I sighed. 'But he killed two Yankees first!' I added with enthusiasm.

The old white-haired man grew animated. 'Hear that, Al?' Then he said to me proudly, 'My grand-daddy lost an eye at the Battle of Kinston.' Willoughby jabbed the sand excitedly with his cane. 'And we won that —'

'Papa, we'd better start back,' the son-in-law interrupted, taking the old man's arm.

'Don't interrupt me, Al,' Willoughby said peevishly, jerking his arm free. 'Al here don't give a damn about southern history, young lady,' he explained. '*His* people are Italians, from Indiana.'

'Illinois,' Al said. 'But I grew up in Florida, Papa.'

'Florida don't count,' snapped Mr. Willoughby. He winked at me. 'Full of Yankees and foreigners.'

I smiled and nodded, then changed the topic. 'You must be heartbroken over this loss,' I said sympathetically, gesturing at the ruins.

He nodded solemnly. 'Bad investment, yes indeed. I was just getting ready to put it up for sale. Nothing left to sell,' he added bitterly, shaking his head.

'Oh yes there is!' I said reassuringly. 'Like that bathtub, and this marble table.' I pointed them out. 'I would love to own these.'

'What for?' He studied me closely.

'Because they're old and they're lovely.' I smiled at him. 'They remind me of the Old South. Of my home state,' I added. 'Mr. Willoughby, I'd like to retire here some day, sir — here in my native state.' I paused. 'In fact, sir, if you want to sell this lot, I'd like to buy it.' I looked at him — well, with sweet sadness, I guess. I was playing him like a fish, so desperate was I to get the land.

'Young lady,' he said, patting my arm, 'I like you. And I'll tell you what —'

'Papa, you need to think this over,' Al interrupted, grabbing Willoughby's arm. 'Let's eat lunch first, talk this over.'

'Alfonso!' Willoughby snapped, jerking his arm away. 'Leave me be! It ain't your property. Now Miss Westmoreland,' he continued, 'if you'll give me just a little more than the insurance value, why —'

Again the son-in-law stopped him. 'Papa, don't take the first offer! Think about the value of the land,' he pleaded.

'I *am* thinking about the land, Al! Look at it! Sand! Just sand. Miss Westmoreland,' he added gently, 'you know there could be another hurricane — next week, next year.'

'I know.' I nodded. 'But I survived this one. Although I lost my car and —'

'You were here?' he interrupted with interest. 'During Hazel?'

I related my narrow escape from the island. He listened sympathetically, nodding and shaking his head. 'My, my,' he said when I concluded. 'Thank the good Lord you were spared.'

'Papa,' Al whined, 'let's you and me talk in private a minute. Selling this land is a big decision. You need my advice before —'

'Alfonso, hush!' Willoughby jabbed his cane into the sand. 'I don't need any more of your financial advice! You talked me into buying this property, back in forty-five, remember? Now look what's left!' He waved his cane at the rubble.

'But think about the future, Papa,' Al pleaded. 'Think about the land, not the house. If you'll just wait a few years —'

'I don't *have* a few years, and you know it,' the old man said loudly. 'I want some cash in my hands right now! Want to take Adele to the Holy Land while we can both still walk. Now just hush up and leave us be!' He waved him away with his cane. 'Go on back to the camp. Go eat!'

The son-in-law shrugged, threw up his hands, and walked away, peevishly kicking a broken board halfway up the low dune.

Mr. Willoughby sighed, shaking his head. 'That boy — he cares about nothing but his belly and his billfold. Now tell me, what church do you attend?'

We ate lunch together at the camp. Willoughby questioned me in detail about my family, my job, my salary, my 'ancestor' at the Fort Fisher battle. I was very thankful I was a southerner, if not a North Carolinian, and had been reared a Protestant.

I hated the lies, Laura! And I lied no more than was absolutely necessary, and I was totally honest about my job and my finances. Most of all I hated the pretense of the Southern Belle, but I feared I might lose the property if I did not play out this role. I *had* to get this site of Selene's cottage!

Willoughby asked me, 'How come you've not got a husband — a pretty, smart young lady like you?'

I clenched my fists under the table. But I smiled modestly and said, 'It's very hard to find a true gentleman, with the right background.'

'A southern gentleman, yes.' He nodded sympathetically.

'Yes indeed. A man of background, and breeding. Like my father — and like you.' I smiled shyly again.

He beamed and patted my hand. 'You stick to those values, young lady,' he said. Then a slight frown crossed his face. 'No, don't *you* ever settle for just anybody.' I knew he was thinking of his daughter and her choice, Al, the mid-western Italian.

We ended our interview with a verbal agreement and a handshake, all that was necessary, I knew. The formality of signing the papers would come later. So when I left him that afternoon, I was confident that this land on the shore, so sacred to Selene and to me, would once more be ours.

I was at the site again well before sunset that day, filled with anticipation. The late afternoon was clear and rather cold, but I was warmly dressed in wool slacks and a heavy, hooded jacket. For a while I explored the ruins, thinking happily about how much I would be able to salvage. I caressed the half-buried tub lovingly.

On the low dune before the cottage ruins was a big chunk of asphalt, once a piece of the road. I sat on this and watched the sunset with mounting excitement. When the moon became dimly visible and the first star appeared, I laughed out loud with glee.

As the twilight deepened, I ran impulsively down to the water's edge. I raced and twirled about on the hard-packed sand like a child, bursting with excitement. Many times I yelled out Selene's name as I ran and jumped and twirled on the isolated beach. And then, my heart pounding, I stopped, stood still, and gazed at the moon's sparkling path across the undulating waves, growing brighter each moment.

I heard behind me, 'Josephine.'

I whirled around, rushed into her waiting arms, crying out with joy. I fell upon her smooth neck with kisses, feeling her pulse throb warmly against my lips. I sobbed, and she kissed my salty tears and murmured, 'Yes, beloved, I am truly here, and you are truly awake. Fear not.'

She took my hand and led me up to the ruins of the cottage. We sat together on the asphalt slab, gazing at the debris. 'This is our place in your world,' she said solemnly. 'Hecate has tried to destroy it, from spite.'

'Hazel,' I said. 'The hurricane was named Hazel.'

She shook her head slowly. 'Hecate,' she repeated softly.

I felt suddenly light-headed, strange. 'But Hecate does not —'

Selene put an arm around me and pulled me close. 'Do not fear,' she whispered. 'Soon you will understand.'

I looked into her lovely, moonlit face. Her deep, dark eyes glittered brilliantly in the sunlight. Hesitantly, almost fearfully, I asked where she had been during the hurricane and during the weeks since then, and I told her of my dreams of her which had guided me back to this spot. I trembled as my confusing thoughts poured from me.

She took my hands. 'You are bewildered and afraid now,' she said. 'But I am real, even as you are. And I am here.'

'How can you read my thoughts?' I blurted out. 'Who — what are you? Where are you from?' My throat tightened, my temples pounded.

She stood and looked down at me, her pale gown and cloak gleaming in the moonlight. She placed her hands on my shoulders and gazed into my eyes deeply. 'Josephine,' she said solemnly, 'believe in me. Know that all I speak to you is true. Know that I love you. Believe these things, and I will be with you forever. Believe in me and you will not know death.' Her eyes glowed brightly.

I stared at her speechless, her strange words ringing in my ears. She cradled my face in her warm slender hands and kissed my forehead. 'Believe in me, and in our love,' she whispered, 'and you will never die.'

I gazed in amazement! I doubted her sanity, and my own. And yet deep within my soul I longed to believe her words.

'Your heart believes,' she said with a smile. 'It is permitted now to reveal the first mysteries to you.'

Aware again of her power to see into my soul, I felt my doubt and fear dissolving. Some force deep within told me her every word was a drop of pure light, a flawless pearl of truth I must grasp and hold forever. I seized her hands and kissed them passionately.

'Believe this first truth,' she said. 'These hands you kiss will never age and die.'

I looked up wide-eyed, speechless.

She smiled at me radiantly. 'Believe this truth, and you will become as I am — your hands, your face, your self unchanging. Even as I am, so shall you become, if you believe in me.'

I gasped, my heart pounding. She pulled me gently to my feet. I felt within me a surge of energy and faith. The radiance about her from the moonlight seemed even brighter.

'You do believe,' she said. 'And to strengthen your faith, it is now permitted to reveal one proof of my words. Come.'

She led me to the edge of the ocean's surf. There she pointed to a small dark object in the wet sand. 'What do you see here?' she asked.

I stooped and examined it. 'A fish,' I answered. I touched it lightly with my foot. 'A dead flounder.'

She took me by the shoulders and gazed at me. 'Disbelieve that it is dead,' she said, 'and it will live! Concentrate! *Order* the fish, in your mind, to live.' Her dark eyes reached my soul.

For some moments I concentrated on the lifeless fish, half doubting her words, yet yearning to believe them. Thinking I saw some slight movement of the tail fin, I tensed with excitement and squeezed Selene's hand.

'Remember this truth,' said Selene insistently. 'Whatever is believed is real! Believe now this creature lives, even as before you believed the dog would live. Will it into life!'

I summoned all my mental energies with growing conviction. The fish twitched, flopped over, then swam into an incoming wave! I stared, shouted, and fell into her arms in joyful amazement!

More mysteries were revealed to me that night and the next two nights we shared together on the solitary beach before the site of our cottage. Repeatedly Selene warned me: 'Because you are still a mortal, often will you be tempted to disbelieve. And if you do, you will age and die like all mortals. Hecate will take you.'

Earnestly I said to her, 'Forever I will believe in you! For if I do not, I know I will lose my very will to live.'

Laura paused. *Forever I will believe in you! For if I do not, I know I will lose my very will to live.*

This was it, Laura thought sadly — the source of Josie's mental illness. Marian's death — Josie had barely survived that, had then almost lost her will to live. And then the brief, exciting new romance on Hatteras Island — a rekindling of Josie's spirit, a new hope, a new reason to live. But Josie had lost too the lovely foreigner, Selene. Lost her in the hurricane, probably to death, Laura thought sadly.

Two losses in two years. Josie had not been able to accept this second loss, had denied it. Laura shook her head. Oh Josie, she thought, you kept this second lover alive! Alive in your mind. And so that you might never lose her, you made your Selene immortal! You *had* to, to keep yourself alive.

Laura sighed, almost near tears. Then she read on:

Selene and I walked and talked together for hours each night on the beach. That first night I asked her to come with me to the camp, to my tent, that I might make love to her.

'It is not permitted,' she said sadly. 'We may not love together fully again, in your waking life, until you have recreated the cottage that was.'

Stunned, dismayed, I stared at her in disbelief. 'Not permitted? But why?' I demanded, filled with desire and frustration.

We were seated on the asphalt slab near the ruins. She took my hands and kissed them gently. Her brilliant black eyes were filled with love and sorrow. 'The gift of immortality,' she explained, 'may never be granted lightly. It is a rare and precious gift which must be earned. There are rules that must be obeyed, tasks that must be performed, trials of faith that must be endured. The Immortal Council has decreed that you must first fulfill this task of recreating the cottage before we may again love together fully in your waking life.'

Seeing my pain and disappointment at these words, she put her arms about me lovingly. 'Be not dismayed, beloved,' she said, her voice brightening. 'In your sleeping life, I will be with you each month, at the time of the full moon, wherever on this planet you might be. Then will our souls reunite in love.'

I rested my head on her shoulder. 'You will come to me in dreams, then, as you did last night?' I asked.

'It was no dream, beloved,' she whispered, kissing my cheek softly. 'I will be with you so and love you eleven moons of each year.'

'Eleven? But there are —'

'Our twelfth moon of each year, your October moon, we will be together in your waking life,' she said. 'Here — on this site of our earthly home, during the three nights of the moon's fullness.' She stroked my face and smiled into my eyes. 'As together we are now, so shall we be each October moon. And when the house is again as it was, again may we love fully there, as before.'

I found hope and strength in her words. 'To be with you eternally,' I said, 'I'll obey any decree. I will rebuild the cottage.' I paused. 'But what is the Immortal Council?'

She smiled and arose, taking my hand. 'It is the supreme power of my world. Seek now to know no more. Believe in me, and obey the decree of the Council. In time more truths will be revealed to you.'

On our second night together, as we walked arm in arm upon the deserted strand, she said to me, 'Earth years must pass before you may see the full light, lest it blind you. Your transformation to the substance that is mine comes not at an instant. Your immortal self is now like the child in the mortal womb. It must evolve in stages to its full maturity.'

'My immortal self is not yet born?' I asked, puzzled.

She shook her head, smiling. 'Birth and death are mortal words. I speak to you figuratively. As your immortal self strengthens, my words will be more clear to you. This much now you will understand — each October, truths will be revealed to you, as your immortal self emerges. And in the twenty-eighth October, the pure radiance will be revealed to you — as the earthly butterfly breaks forth from the darkness of the shell and soars up into the light.'

Dearest Laura, I wish I could reveal to you all I learned then — and since! But the Immortal Council does not permit me to tell you all. I may tell you this: Thousands of earth years ago, many came from Selene's world to this planet, hoping to bring the light of truth to humanity. But the results were disastrous. The ancient Greeks and Romans who they visited, in Selene's words, 'saw with imperfect eyes.' So they wrote much about the

106

Immortals that was false, and few mortals proved worthy of their gift of immortality.

Selene told me about Mount Cynthus, explaining, 'Never do I speak falsely to you. I told you I was incarnated there. That is true. There I first took on this mortal form. But birth and death I do not know. These events belong to your mortal world, not mine.'

She explained her name as one of several given her by ancient mortals. 'The name on your earth I like best,' she said. 'Some call me Cynthia, however, after the place of my incarnation, but the Cynthia who loved the mortal Endymion was not I, though her love for him was much like mine for you.'

'Explain more to me about Hecate,' I said. 'Is she too an Immortal?'

At this question Selene shook her head sadly. 'Hecate is false, and yet the source of all earthly woe. The mortal mind created Hecate and gave her great power. To become as I am, you must disbelieve in Hecate! If all mortals would disbelieve in her, she would vanish.'

She spoke gravely and slowly. 'Among the many errors recorded by your ancients was this belief in Hecate. Even worse, a false confusion of her with me, or with Cynthia. These imperfect philosophers of old associated me with the bright side of your moon, and Hecate with the dark side. When the moon was full, they believed that I was then in power, the force of life. When the moon vanished from their sight, they believed then that Hecate was in power, the force of death.'

'How could they confuse such an opposite being with you?' I asked, gazing at her radiant beauty.

'Even as the moon for your earth is one object, they concluded that Hecate and I were one — the two sides of mortality, life and death.' She sighed. 'Such misery for mortals has come from this false belief! Hecate is not real! Yet mortals believe she exists, believe that darkness and age and death exist. And because they believe so, they have made it so! Remember this truth, beloved: whatever is believed is real.'

We sat now on the asphalt seat before the site of our cottage. She put her arms about me and drew me near. 'Even before I chose you as the mortal I would love, I knew your love of me would be stronger than your fear of Hecate. I knew you would prove worthy.'

I looked at her surprised. 'You loved me before you came to me? And knew I would love you? And believe in you?'

She told me she had loved me since my childhood, because of my unchanging belief in the goodness and beauty of all life. And that when Hecate had taken from me the mortal woman who was my beloved, she had felt my pain in her immortal soul. 'I feared you might fall,' Selene said, 'into Hecate's web of despair. My love for you deepened then and I sought the Council's permission to be incarnated before you and seek you as my beloved.'

The small dog in the sea had been a test of my worthiness. 'I created this creature,' she explained, 'seeming to be in danger, in Hecate's hands.'

'Was the dog then a mere illusion?' I asked, rapt.

'No,' she said firmly. 'As I told you before, she is now in her own element — dwelling forever among the Immortals. Nothing made immortal can be destroyed.'

Remembering how I had finally fled the sea, I said with shame, 'I wanted the dog to live, yes. But surely I failed this test . . .'

'You did not fail,' she said gently, taking my hands. 'Death by drowning has always been your greatest fear.

Yet you entered the water, at what you believed was a deadly risk, proving your reverence for all life. Thus did you prove your strong desire still to believe in me, not the false Hecate.'

'It was the same dog as in the dream!' I exclaimed. 'The one that jumped out of the fish pail.'

'Yes.' She smiled. 'All in that vision was true. I came to you first in your sleeping life, to prepare you for my incarnation at the October moon and these truths I now reveal to you.'

On our third night that November, Selene revealed to me how I would become as she was, immortal. 'Never forget,' she warned, 'that Hecate will continue to tempt you. If you yield to her, you will be lost!'

I expressed my surprise that Hecate could have such power. 'You've said she's not real,' I said. 'How can she be so strong then, and a danger to me?'

'Never forget,' Selene replied, 'that whatever is believed is real. Belief in death is the strongest belief in your world. The energy of this collective belief is enormously powerful. It created Hecate. It sustains her. It makes possible the mortal miseries of age, decay, and death. All these are manifestations of Hecate's power, given to her by the mortal mind.'

'What of the natural disasters?' I asked, grimly remembering Hazel.

'These too are all the work of Hecate. Your world believes these will happen,' she explained. 'This collective belief makes them so.'

To achieve my immortality, she explained, I had to resist the power of Hecate. 'Your mind,' she said solemnly, 'must fight against a great power — the collective force of billions of mortal minds.'

109

I felt helpless at this requirement. 'How can I win in such a struggle?' I asked. 'How can my mind alone defeat such power?'

Her bright eyes burned with determination. 'You *will* defeat it,' she said confidently. 'For you will have my help, my power — always!' Her eyes grew brighter, her face more radiant. 'Know that I will be with you always, though you see me only at the fullness of your earthly moon. Think of me always. Write of me, and of these truths, in your journals.'

She looked at me gravely and gripped my hands. 'But share this knowledge with no mortal! To do so would be great danger!' She explained that speaking of her and my coming immortality would strengthen Hecate's powers. 'The mortals would laugh at you, call you insane,' she said, 'but secretly envy you. Then they would try to destroy your belief in me, so that you would yield like them to age and death. Thus might you be taken by Hecate. And lost to me.'

I shivered and hugged her tight, remembering my nightmare of that cold, bony hand seizing my shoulder in the darkness. Selene wrapped me in her arms, stroking my hair.

'Prepare for this also,' she said gently. 'In this time of transformation you must appear to age as do all mortals, lest our secret be revealed. But do not let this mere illusion shake your belief in me and your evolving immortality. Your immortal self will grow in strength and beauty even as your mortal shell appears to weaken.'

She kissed my brow tenderly. 'Never fear this surface illusion might lessen my love for you, beloved Josephine,' she murmured. 'Your mortal shell is never what I see. Always I see the immortal you — the self that left this

110

shell and came to me at the fireplace that first evening.'
She looked into my eyes and smiled lovingly.

Curious, I asked, 'What does my immortal self look like to you?' When she replied that this self looked like the physical self I then saw in my mirrors, I was puzzled. 'My immortal self will always be this age?' I asked. 'I will be forty-two forever?'

She smiled at me as if I were an infant. 'You will be no age,' she said, brushing back my hair.

I asked her then about the World of the Immortals and how she would take me there.

'The Moment of Passage I have told you,' she answered. 'Remember your immortal self is now but in its infancy. Be patient. Not yet can you bear the light of fuller revelations.'

CHAPTER FOUR
Sunday, 2:00 A.M., October 10

Dear God, Laura thought sadly. Many years of deepening psychosis, and she herself, a psychologist, had never even suspected it. She grew increasingly angry at herself. Why hadn't she seen the signs? Josie's rejection of clocks, watches — her denial of *time*. The mysterious "young friend" Josie had begun mentioning in recent years, the "wine maker" — no wonder Josie "couldn't arrange" for anyone to meet her.

Laura marked her place in the manuscript and put it on the coffee table. Exhausted in mind and body, she could read no further.

She tossed restlessly in Josie's bed, fearfully anticipating what the rest of the manuscript would reveal. She fought against the feeling that she had somehow failed Josie. The illness had begun, after all, three decades ago, with Marian's death. Laura's parents hadn't seen it, nor Larry's either. The disease had been far advanced when Laura was only a child. Growing up with a middle-aged aunt the adult world saw as just somewhat eccentric, how could Laura have seen strangeness in what to her had always been normal behavior, for Josie?

And the disease had been so well hidden, so unapparent. Like a cancer undetected until too late. Perhaps never detected, had there not been Josie's manuscript. Laura paused, grief welling up within her. Even if Josie was still alive somewhere, she was truly lost. Laura almost hoped they would find her dead. That sight of Josie might be more bearable than the sight of her hopelessly sick.

Struggling to sleep, listening to the muffled moaning of the breakers on the beach, she felt her sadness and solitude intensely. She thought again of Jackie — and her loving eyes.

A rainy Saturday in April floated into her memory. The two of them on the living room rug in Jackie's apartment, playing with the little mixed-breed puppy Jackie had just adopted that morning at the SPCA. Jackie on her jeaned knees, studying the lively puppy through her camera. The fat-bellied, brown and white puppy fiercely shaking an old blue sock it had found in the bedroom, ignoring Jackie's offer of a squeaky rubber hamburger.

"I can't believe," Jackie had said, laughing, "you conned me into adopting this crazy little fuzzball."

"Conned you?" Laura protested. "It was either her or the Saint Bernard!"

"I was only kidding about the Saint Bernard."

"Kidding my foot! If I hadn't pointed out —"

"Okay, okay," Jackie interrupted, her teeth flashing in a grin. "You were right — he'd have needed a shovel-sized pooper scooper." She grabbed the dog, which was now attacking her jeans. "Hey, hey! No!" she yelled, holding it close to her face. "We do not eat Mommy's jeans," she lectured. She released the puppy, which ran directly to Laura and began licking her hands.

"Tragically deranged," Jackie said with mock gravity. She stretched out, leaning back on her elbows, watching the dog adore Laura. "Totally crazy. There was a prophetic sign," she added with a sigh, "but I did not heed it."

"You mean when she wet in the car?" Laura asked, tossing the blue sock which the puppy chased.

"Nah, not that." Jackie looked at her with a twinkle in her brown eyes. "After all, it was *your* car."

"You rat!" Laura lunged at her and shoved her playfully. "So what was your prophetic sign of her craziness?"

"As soon as the attendant opened the cage, this nutty fuzz-ball went directly to *you*!"

"Crazy, huh? For loving me?" Laura threw the rubber hamburger at Jackie.

"Yep! Crazy." Jackie laughed, dodging the toy, then paused. "Like her new mama," she had added, her tone suddenly different, almost sad.

114

"You were trying to tell me then," Laura whispered into the darkness.

Finally Laura slipped into a fitful sleep. She dreamed that Jackie's puppy was drowning in the ocean while she watched from the shore, paralyzed. She heard Jackie's voice calling to her in the darkness; she groped blindly for Jackie in the blackness.

Laura's eyes flew open. She was lying on her side, facing the painting of Cynthia and Endymion, illuminated in the darkness. The eyes of the sleeping Endymion slowly opened, stared at her with milky, blind pupils, which then dissolved into empty black sockets. The arm extended toward the circle in the sand withered, disintegrated into dust.

Laura tried to scream but could not. Cynthia lifted her downcast eyes, riveted them evilly upon Laura, leered at her with lips curled back in a triumphant sneer, hissed "*Hecate!*" The face twisted hideously, whitened. The long hair moved, curled, became a mass of writhing snakes. Laughing insanely, the monster flew out from the picture and onto Laura, seizing Laura's shoulders with ice-cold skeletal hands, again shrieking "*Hecate!*"

Screaming her terror, Laura sat up and stared wild-eyed into the darkness, gasping, trembling.

Silence — broken only by the soft ticking of her travel alarm on the bedside table, her own heavy breathing, the distant pounding of the surf. She fell back onto the bed. For some time she stared blankly through the thin-curtained window at the star-filled sky. Then she drifted again into sleep.

It was twelve-fifteen when she woke again. For a while she just lay there. Then, with a sigh, she got up and dressed.

In the living room she found a note slipped under the beachfront door:

Sorry I missed you. I'll stop by again after supper. Found out about the picture. Cynthia was the goddess of the moon, in Greek myths. The young man was a mortal she loved. She visited him in his sleep. The affair ended tragically. No further news. Bill Tate.

The affair ended tragically. Laura sighed, shook her head. Selene and Josie, she thought — like Cynthia and Endymion. The painting in the bedroom had only reinforced Josie's obsession. Laura crumpled the note and threw it into the stove.

She heated some canned soup, ate it mechanically. Finally, reluctantly, coffee mug in hand, she returned to the couch and Josie's story:

Now you will begin to understand everything, dear Laura. I am one of the chosen! Selene's love for me was so strong that she took the great risk of the incarnation and the offer of immortality. There was great danger for her as well as me in this choice. If my belief in her should fail, if Hecate should take me, then Selene would exist forever in great sadness. An Immortal chooses but one beloved. If that choice is mortal and the mortal fails to reach the Moment of Passage, the Immortal suffers the loss of that beloved forever. While I remained in this earthly world, as I must until the maturity of my immortal self, Hecate would be an ever-present danger to us. And as her powers strengthened each month with the waning of the moon, so did Selene's weaken in this world. This was the meaning

116

of the words in my first vision about veiling and penance. If Selene lost me to Hecate, she would for all time afterwards live in mourning and in a solitude which she likened to that of the sequestered earthly nun.

Choosing me meant also agreeing to those restrictions decreed by the Immortal Council which I have already explained to you. Selene had been allowed the November incarnation so that she might explain to me these things I have now revealed to you.

My task of reconstructing our cottage was crucial. It would demonstrate my belief in Selene, her world, and our love, as well as helping assure my transformation.

After our joyful November reunion, I returned to Richmond and began planning for this great task, which I viewed not as a burden, but an act of love and great pleasure. I knew this task would be difficult for me financially, given my modest Post Office salary, and it would take a number of years to complete. But I welcomed this chance to demonstrate my love and my belief.

Every weekend and holiday I devoted to this task. From the rubble of the old cottage I salvaged all I could. Not merely fixtures and furniture, such as the bathtub and marble tables, but also bits and pieces of the house itself. I exulted over each usable board or shingle, treasured each doorknob and unbent nail.

I wrote to old Mr. Willoughby, asking if he remembered certain details about the house. His response was a most marvelous gift — the blueprints of the original house!

Once construction began, I supervised most diligently. I expect the workmen dreaded the sight of my car on those week days I took leave-time from the Post Office and arrived at the site almost as soon as they did. And of course I had my October vacation. I brought a tent and sleeping bag and camped at the site.

Selene assisted in my task. Whenever memory of some detail failed me — such as how many panes of glass there had been in a particular window — I would write down this question. And when next she was with me, either in my sleeping life or in my waking life, I would put such questions to her. She also helped in duplicating those furnishings not salvageable or lost entirely — such as the couch and Morris chair. She drew sketches for me to give to the craftsmen and provided details about the woods and fabrics.

Our great enemy, Hecate, hampered the reconstruction several times, jealously hurling storms she hoped would prevent, delay, or even destroy the construction. When the house was but a skeletal frame, for instance, she sent Hurricane Gracie to shake its timbers. But the damage was slight. The pilings, flooring and wall studs stood firm. The diabolical witch then retreated for a while. I watched excitedly as the cottage reached completion during the spring and summer of that sixth year, 1960.

During one of Selene's visits to me in my sleeping life late that August, when all that remained was to move the furnishings into the house, Selene warned of another impending assault from Hecate. 'In but half a moon's time,' she said solemnly, 'Hecate will brew a fierce storm, far to the south. She will send it first through the islands called the Keys. Then she will send it north, to destroy again our earthly home.'

Angered at this news, I shouted, 'How dare she? How *dare* she?' Looking desperately at Selene I added, 'Surely your power will prevent this!'

'My power, and yours,' she replied, 'will prevent loss of our home, yes. But not some damage to it. Remember the power of the collective mortal mind, which feeds her strength.'

'What must I do?' I asked.

'Go there a week before this time and prepare for her assault. And delay placing the household goods within until afterwards.' She kissed me reassuringly. 'The harm will be slight,' she said.

I remember well how beautiful a day it was on the sixth of September, how placid the sea, as I shuttered the windows and nailed strong boards over these. A local fisherman on the beach looked at me most strangely, no doubt thinking me mad. But as Selene had predicted, the next week Hurricane Donna struck the Florida Keys, then regathered her strength at sea, followed the east coast northward, and struck the Outer Banks on September 12, 1960. Damage to the Banks was heavy. But our cottage lost only a few shingles. These were quickly replaced and the furnishings moved in by the end of the month.

There would be other storms, other hurricanes, for Hecate would continue her vain attempts to destroy my belief in Selene and make me subject to herself. But Selene and I, and the cottage, would weather these and emerge in triumph, even from the two September hurricanes — Cleo in 1964 and David in 1979 — which Hecate hoped would thwart our October reunions.

After Hurricane Hazel, however, as you probably know, Laura, the subsequent hurricanes on the Outer Banks grew progressively weaker, and fewer. Was this not so because of Selene's presence in this place, and her power? I *know* that it was!

Everything was complete for the October reunion in 1960. As always, I arrived at the cottage shortly before the time of the full moon. As you might imagine, I was filled to excess with intense excitement! For six years I had yearned for this moment when we would again be together not only on the beach, but before the fireplace — and in our bed. I anticipated Selene's arrival as if her incarnated form were still an unveiled mystery.

I must confess feeling some slight anxiety as I viewed myself in the bedroom mirror. I well understood the necessity of my surface aging, but had not yet adjusted comfortably to this mere illusion. My mortal shell was now forty-eight, the hair graying, the flesh less firm. Remembering Selene's unchanging beauty and youth, I fought against a growing fear my body might repel Selene, feared too I might yet be lost to Hecate, and age and die like all mortals.

But I soon dismissed these dreadful thoughts, knowing them sent by Hecate to weaken me. I then concentrated my energies on the cottage's interior. It was crucial everything be precisely as before. I rearranged the couch pillows, refolded the afghans, positioned and repositioned the Morris chair during this interval, which seemed to grow longer as the time grew nearer to the moment of Selene's return.

Selene had said to me once, 'Though the writings of mortals are imperfect, some reflect beauty and truth.' Many times in those last hours I reread a sonnet by John Keats, 'Bright Star,' which I would recite to her on this special occasion. I knew she would be pleased by the opening of it — 'Bright star, would I were steadfast as thou art' — and would like very much the closing lines:

... still steadfast, still unchangeable,
　Pillow'd upon my fair love's ripening breast,
To feel for ever its soft swell and fall,
　Awake for ever in a sweet unrest,
Still, still to hear her tender-taken breath,
And so live ever — or else swoon to death.

It saddened me that Keats had fallen victim to Hecate in his youth. But it delighted me that he had left this poem so beautifully capturing what he had longed for, what *I* would achieve! Yes, *I* would be forever 'pillow'd upon my fair love's ripening breast' — forever with Selene!

On the eve of her incarnation, I left the cottage before sunset. I climbed the dunes and watched the sun set over Pamlico Sound just as I had that first October. I recalled every detail of that time — wading into the icy sea to rescue the dog, shivering behind the dunes. Again I visualized Selene's beauty as she stood at the crest of the dunes.

I watched the moon rise over the Atlantic, palely reflecting the pastel colors of the sunset. Oh! How my excitement mounted! I knew Selene would appear this time at the cottage, not on the beach, and I went there quickly now as twilight deepened. My hand shaking with anticipation, I lit the tall pale candle on the round table between the oceanfront windows, as she had said I must do. No sooner had I blown out the match than, behind me, I heard Selene's voice — 'I am here, my beloved Josephine.' I turned and fell joyfully into her arms.

She kissed me deeply and pulled me close. I felt the soft rise and fall of her breasts against my breasts. She stroked my hair softly and murmured, 'Well done, my beloved. This earthly home we will now share each October, until your Moment of Passage.'

I kissed and caressed her with mounting desire. Then she pulled back from me. Her dark eyes brightened. Smiling at me, she removed her pale yellow gown and stood before me once again in the fullness of her beauty.

I wept with joy. Overwhelmed by her loveliness and my deep desire for her, I fell to my knees. Gently, reverently, with trembling hands slowly I began to explore her smooth, warm flesh.

She stopped me. 'Not yet.' She smiled. 'These delights we must know later. First, you must see your reward!' She pulled me to my feet. 'Come with me now to our bedchamber,' she whispered.

At the bedroom door I hesitated. 'Have no fear,' Selene said softly. 'She cannot touch you, for I am here, and at the full.'

I seized her hands and looked into her bright dark eyes. She held out her arms to me. 'Come to me, beloved,' she murmured, pulling me gently into her arms. 'Know that I am real. *Believe* in me!' she whispered urgently.

I held fast to her, feeling my faith stirring, swelling, growing. I pressed hard against her, my fears ebbing.

'Yes, beloved, *yes*,' she urged. 'Come *into* me! Self into self, soul into soul!'

As when a wave sweeps up suddenly and wipes a footprint from the sand, annihilating in an instant this illusion of mortality, so did the splendor of her self sweep through me. Dissolving all doubt, sweeping into nothingness all fear. I sobbed with rapture and collapsed panting into her arms.

For some time she soothed me with gentle hands and loving kisses. Then, as I regained my power of speech, calmer now and confident, my soul filled with love and joy and knowledge, I cried out, '*Never* will I yield to Hecate! *Forever* will I believe in *you!*' I broke off, sobbing from this ecstasy of total union of our immortal selves — a union my mortal words can only shadow, render merely in mortal figures, human images, dear niece.

Selene began to gently remove my sweater and blouse. 'Look first here, my beloved,' she said, continuing to undress me. 'The mirror will show but your higher self.'

I stepped from my slacks. I stared amazed at each spot where she pointed. 'Here there was a wound to your knee,' she said. 'And here to your foot.'

'Gone!' I shouted. 'Vanished!' The scars from my biking accident had totally disappeared. I hugged her, kissed her with gratitude, laughed loudly.

'Such damages to your mortal shell touch not your self,' she said. 'See now the self I always see!' She kissed my forehead, then released me.

I raced to the bedroom mirror, stared into it, cried out with joy! My face was firmer, younger. The gray had vanished from my hair. I turned and fell into Selene's arms, almost fainting from excitement. 'Forty-two again!' I sobbed.

'No age,' she reminded me, rocking me in her arms. 'Time touches us not, beloved. This you must always remember.'

I looked again at the reflection of my immortal self. I swept back my bangs, studied my forehead. 'The mole that came here last year, even it's gone!' I laughed triumphantly.

'Never was it on your immortal self,' she said. 'But you will see it again, in the morning. On your mortal shell.'

I sighed. 'Sometimes I wish —'

She stopped me with a kiss, then said gravely, 'Ask for no more at present, beloved. Be patient. Remember the dangers.'

I nodded and trembled slightly. I could still be lost to Hecate or denied the Council's final gift of eternity with Selene in the Place of the Immortals. 'Yes, I will be patient,' I said to her solemnly. 'The restrictions of the Council are wise.'

She smiled at me proudly. 'Your mortal form will appear to age and weaken these earth years, except when I am with you. Those nights only may you see your immortal self.'

'But after the Moment of Passage —'

'Beloved, in earth centuries hence, this period of your transformation and testing will be to your memory shorter than the blinking of an eye. Eons beyond all time, for all eternity, still will we be together — like this!'

She turned me to face the mirror again. She stood behind me, her arms lovingly circling my waist. And we laughed as we looked together at the images of our immortal selves — united, as we always would be.

Surprised by her feelings, Laura stopped reading. She reread this scene and found herself smiling — not grimly, not bitterly, but warmly. But why? Then she realized that Josie's life had after all been enormously happy in these latter years. Why should I be saddened by her sickness, Laura asked herself, if it made Josie so very happy? This obsession with an imagined woman-turned-goddess, had it not given Josie great joy — a joy she might otherwise not have had? Had this belief in an immortal lover, and in Josie's own immortality, really been destructive? Or had this madness not, after all, enabled her to live happily in a world in which, all too often, bitterness, even despair, became the lot of shy, lonely, aging women like her?

Laura looked again at the scene of Josie and Selene hugging and laughing before the mirror. It triggered memory of an afternoon in late May with Jackie.

They had been shopping for bathing suits. Later, in Laura's apartment, Laura put on her new suit and studied herself critically before the full-length bedroom mirror.

"I'm getting old and flabby," she grumbled. "Just look at these thighs!" She glanced from her reflection to Jackie's.

Sitting behind Laura on the bed, Jackie said, smiling, "You look great to me."

Laura smoothed her suit across her abdomen and sighed. "I weigh the same as last summer. But everything's shifting . . . or something." She frowned at her reflection.

Jackie got up then, and slipped her arms around Laura's waist from behind. Addressing her in the mirror, Jackie said, "The Laura I see hasn't changed one bit. And she never will," she added firmly. "Not in my eyes. To me you'll always be beautiful." The big brown eyes met Laura's in the mirror with an expression that warmed Laura. An open look of absolute admiration and devotion. A look of love, Laura now realized.

Laura had turned then, returned Jackie's hug. But then she laughed, pulled away, said something silly: "I hope Bruce is as blind as you are!"

Jackie's smooth handsome face had paled slightly, her eyes darkening.

At the time, Laura had thought only that Jackie did not think Bruce good enough for her. Now she knew the pain in Jackie's face had come from a deeper source, her special love for Laura.

Bruce's reaction to Laura in the new bathing suit had been typical: "Not bad," said with a shrug, "but you could stand to lose a few pounds."

How could he, she thought now, stand there with his balding head and his beer belly, and demand of her a physical perfection he felt not at all compelled to seek in himself? Why had she endured Bruce Watts for three long years? She felt angry again that she had ever been involved with him.

"To me you'll always be beautiful," Jackie had said. What had Jackie seen in the mirror? Just a body in a bathing suit? Or something more? Maybe something like what Josie's Selene saw, and caused Josie to see also.

Bruce Watts was consigned now to her past. But Jackie . . . Three years, Laura thought sadly. Wonderful years when she and Jackie had shared so much, given so much to each other. Never had *they* bored each other, or played stupid power games . . .

Never had she had to *pretend* affection for Jackie, either. What she felt for her was real — deep and vital. It was love, yes. She had loved Jackie . . . still loved her. She missed the laughing, warm brown eyes. The strong white teeth flashing in an almost boyish grin. The hugs, the touches . . . Jackie's strong farmgirl hands, rubbing her back with suntan lotion beside the apartment building's pool.

Laura sighed, her eyes watering. Why, oh why had she driven away this wonderful woman — so caring, so loving? And why did she still ache so much from the loss of her, still long so much to see her, hear her voice? *Why had she ended it?*

The ghost of her own cold words was like an icy knife in her heart: "I can't love you."

"Why didn't you say, '*I don't?*' " she asked her frozen shadow, the cold Laura with folded arms. The realization swelled within her and over her like a tremendous wave. She could not then — and she could not now — say "I don't love you" to Jackie. Because she *did* love her . . . then and now. And with the same kind of love, she realized, that Jackie felt for her.

Almost blinded by her tears, Laura stumbled into the bathroom. Blowing her nose and crying, she looked up at her reflection in the mirror. "I felt it again," she whispered. "Like that time with Margaret." That same secret excitement . . . Maybe that's why she had frozen, shut down. Fear — pure and simple fear.

She wiped her eyes, looked into them. "Like that time with Margaret," she repeated softly, remembering the long-forgotten scene in the dormitory room she had shared with her best friend since high school.

They had been discussing Roy McClain, Laura's steady boyfriend at the University of Virginia since her junior year. Margaret began peeling off her clothes in preparation for her shower. Laura had moved away, toward her bed. "You know, Laurie," Margaret said, stepping out of her panties, her back to Laura, "he's an awful good catch! Pre-med, darling."

127

Laura said nothing, studying her white hips, smooth back, well-shaped legs. Admiring Margaret's loveliness in secret. Margaret turned then and looked at her, smiling. Laura quickly averted her eyes from the nude body.

"I wouldn't pass up this chance to snag him if I were you." Margaret laughed, pulling her thin bathrobe around her. Laura's eyes drifted from Margaret's face to her half-concealed breasts. The nipples were erect against the silky fabric.

"Sometimes, my darling," Margaret continued, "I worry about you." She tossed back her sandy mane, fixed her cat-like eyes on Laura, her smile almost seductive. "If you don't sleep with a man soon . . ." She paused. Laura felt her stomach knotting. Margaret laughed again, her eyes still fixed on Laura's. "Of course *I'd* never really think it," Margaret had continued, "but . . . well, it does seem, don't you think, a bit . . . queer? Still being a virgin, I mean."

"Dammit!" Laura exclaimed all these years later, now realizing she'd sleep with Roy out of fear. Fear of losing Margaret's central presence in her life, a presence threatened by that word *queer*. She had been in love with Margaret, of course, but afraid to admit it.

Then she had met Jean Diaz, a dark brunette with almost black eyes, and like Laura a part-time graduate student in psychology at Virginia Commonwealth University. They soon became close friends. And through Jean she met Donald Evans, Jean's cousin. Laura had endured almost two years of Donald. Because of her devotion to Jean, of course. And that same fear of losing the friendship . . . How absurd it all seemed now. To keep Jean, she kept Donald. Yet the friendship between herself and Jean had slackened anyway, once Jean married.

The pattern was all too clear. Laura washed her tear-stained face, studying her eyes in the mirror. Roy, and Donald — to please Margaret, and Jean. To stay close to these women who secretly excited her. And to hide from them, and from herself, emotions they stirred in her which she feared would cost her their presence.

But why had she panicked with Jackie — frozen up, driven *her* away? It made no sense, she thought, walking back to the living room. Jackie had loved her in a way not possible for Margaret or Jean. Jackie had not used her, had not tried to change her, had not tried to rearrange her life. She had given her a hundred times more real affection, more genuine love, than anyone had ever given her. Had loved her absolutely, with no qualifications. Had finally declared to her what Laura had never allowed herself to articulate — a deep, romantic — yes, physical too — love for another woman.

Laura dropped to the couch, stared at the open manuscript. Suddenly remembering Josie's words in the letter paper-clipped to the first page, she reread the sentence: "We were mortally afraid to be honest."

Afraid to be honest. The words burned into her heart. *That's why I drove Jackie away. Because I was mortally afraid to be honest — honest with myself.*

How ironic. Jackie had loved her back, and she had not been prepared. She had been thrown off balance, forced to face the long-suppressed question: *Am I a lesbian?*

She laughed bitterly through her tears. All those psychology courses, all that training — how ironic. How many homosexual men, some women too, had she counseled, reassuring them in textbook fashion that it was okay to have their feelings, to express them, act on them? Perfectly fine for *them* to be who they were, she always said ... The blind leading the blind!

"Well not any more," she said aloud. She felt better now, knowing what she would do. Telephone Jackie this very night. Try to explain the craziness. Hope she would listen, would understand — maybe even forgive her.

But now ... Now she had to finish Josie's manuscript. Tate would be there in a few more hours. She owed it to Josie, and to herself, to read the rest before then. And besides, she was very curious.

CHAPTER FIVE
Sunday, 4:30 P.M., October 10

Laura returned to Josie's *True Story* with an interest only deepened by her better understanding of Josie, and of herself. Feeling a kinship with Josie beyond mere blood, she read on eagerly:

How can I capture in mortal words the ecstasy of our reunion that October of 1960 — the joy, the completeness, the excitement of it all? It surpassed the beauty, the wonder, the happiness of all reunions we had shared before. I can give you only glimpses, dear niece — mere shadows of this time of perfect joy.

Sometimes Selene and I were like adolescent lovers. Teasing, tickling, racing like fillies on the moonlit beach. We'd do wonderfully silly childlike things — build sand castles, play hide-and-go-seek in the dunes. And we'd make love with shy, innocent freshness and the excitement of novices.

Other times, arms linked, we'd slowly pace the solitary sands at midnight like grave old philosophers, discussing the mysteries of the universe. She was the master teacher, I the ardent pupil. The lessons, the truths I learned then!

I filled my solitary daylight hours as always — writing, thinking of the deep truths Selene had revealed to me, studying the wonders of nature all about me. Napping too, yes. And of course, eagerly anticipating Selene's return at twilight.

The next eight years moved all too slowly for me, eager as I was to leave Richmond. But Selene's visits to me in my sleeping life and our October reunions strengthened me greatly in those years. And 1968 finally arrived: the year of my early retirement from the Post Office, and my permanent move to Hatteras Island.

You'll remember, of course, helping me move here. Larry pulling the little U-Haul with his station wagon, you and I riding behind him in my old Chevrolet. There wasn't very much to haul down here — mainly just books and clothes. Most of the things in the Richmond house I had already sold, along with the house itself. The cottage, Selene's and mine, had long since become our true home, you see.

Moving into our cottage was surpassed only by my October reunion with Selene that year. I was then, in the world's eyes, fifty-six. But as always, my self was unchanged.

For a long time Selene and I stood together nude before our bedroom mirror. Spilling over with joy at the sight of my immortal self in the reflection, I cried out triumphantly, 'Hecate! You are nothing!'

'False she is, yes. But do not boast she is nothing,' Selene warned. 'She will tempt you still, even until your last hour on this planet.'

'But she has no power over me!' I said confidently, turning to face my beloved.

Selene hugged me tightly. 'Guard against pride,' she said anxiously. 'Her power is still great in this realm! She will still fight to take you from me. Even more strongly so now,' she added sadly, 'in these last fourteen earth years to come. Her attacks will be stronger, more subtle. Stay guarded, careful, strong in your faith. Yet humble also in the knowledge of your great gift. Above all things now, fight against pride, which could lead you to boast before mortals, thus increasing her power.'

Rightfully rebuked for my dangerous arrogance, I lowered my eyes in shame. She kissed each eyelid tenderly, then whispered, 'She will not take you, unless you allow it. You have not yielded yet to the attacks upon your mortal shell, which are slight.'

I looked up, nodded, gazed into her brilliant eyes.

'These attacks,' she continued gravely, 'have been frail arrows — the graying of your hair, the weakening of your eyesight, the loss of a few teeth. You know well these attacks upon your mortal shell are harmless. They do not touch your self.' She paused, took my shoulders. 'But now your immortal self has grown through infancy into later childhood. And now will Hecate hurl toward you much stronger spears.'

Selene was right, of course. Hecate doubled, tripled her assaults on me those later earthly years, attacking both directly and indirectly, displaying her power by taking from me people I loved. She sent a fierce storm to destroy the plane which held Larry's parents, claiming them as hers in an instant. Increasingly desperate in her attempts to seize me from Selene by destroying my faith in her, within a year afterwards she took away your mother.

I remember how Selene came to me in my sleeping life that April, no more than a week after your mother's death, Laura. 'I believed!' I sobbed, falling into Selene's arms. 'I believed Ellie would not die! I sat by her bedside and willed her to live, as I had done years ago with the fish lying on the strand. Yet still she died.'

Selene soothed me in my sorrow, stroking my face with tender hands. 'Humans are not like the lesser earth creatures,' she explained gently. 'You may will a fish to live, but not command another mortal to live. Except yourself.' She paused for a moment. 'Eleanor believed in Hecate. She expected to grow ill and die. And so she did. You know that all is real that can be imagined. Do not blame yourself for her fate. You were powerless to change it. Only your own future lies within your power.'

These words strengthened me greatly. Again, with Selene's help, I avoided Hecate's web of despair.

The 1975 October reunion marked the beginning of a crucial phase in our battle with Hecate. That twenty-first reunion was a time of great joy for Selene and me, yet also some sadness. The pain of the loss of Ellie six months earlier was still fresh in my heart. And Hecate's assaults on my human form, now aged sixty-three years, were

134

quite apparent in my totally white hair and wrinkling skin.

But my self was, as always, unchanged. And when Selene was with me, the illusionary mortal shell vanished, as always, and the fleshly image was again as it had been twenty-one years before.

On our third night at the cottage, Selene was unusually animated. As we lay nude before the fireplace, resting after our lovemaking, she teased me playfully, then said, her dark eyes flashing, 'Soon will there be another gift.'

'What?' I sat up on my elbows and looked at her curiously.

She smiled and tossed back her moon-pale hair. 'You will see.' She laughed lightly.

'When?' I grabbed her wrist.

She laughed and pulled free. 'Be patient!' she commanded with mock seriousness.

I lunged at her, pinning her down by her shoulders. 'Tell me!' I ordered, laughing. 'What gift? When?' Then I pulled back and lovingly studied her face in the moonbeams that bathed us.

She rose gracefully, pulled me into her bosom, rocking me. 'It is forbidden to tell you,' she murmured, 'but this gift will come soon. Be patient, my beloved Josephine.'

That morning, as always, on the third morning of our reunion time I awoke to an empty bed. As had been my habit for many years, I wrote in my journal until late afternoon. Then I left the cottage to take my usual long walk on this eve of separation. It was my custom at such times to walk many miles for many hours, to tire myself so much that I would be able to sleep again in solitude. The long hours of pacing the beach lessened too the sadness I always felt on our eves of separation.

The late afternoon was exceptionally warm and peaceful. The sky was cloudless, the wind mild, the ocean serene. The tide was out. I took off my shoes and waded in tide pools, searching for sand dollars, scattering small schools of minnows. I found a lovely conch, the mollusk inside still alive, and returned it to the sea. I could not kill this creature for its home.

As twilight deepened, I walked the strand near the cottage, buried in happy memories of this latest reunion time. I stared often at the moon, watching its hues change as the sun set and the sky darkened. The moon was visibly diminishing now, starting its approach to its half-moon stage. A sadness swept through me as I stared at the weakening moon. I missed Selene terribly.

Something urged me to turn and look at our cottage. I stared with amazement! There behind the front windows, *four* candles were burning brightly! 'Selene!' I cried out as I raced across the sand toward our home.

'Selene! Beloved!' I cried as I burst into the living room. Breathtakingly beautiful in her pale yellow gown, she turned from the table where the candles stood as on an altar and held out her arms to me. I fell into her almost fainting with joy.

This was the wonderful secret, the new gift — a fourth night together in October. The Immortal Council had granted this as a reward for our steadfastness.

'Will this happen again next October?' I asked excitedly.

She smiled and nodded. 'If you cling to your faith, our gifts from the Council will so increase, yes, my beloved. In the earth year preceding your Year of Eternity, our October nights together will number seven.'

'Seven!' I shouted joyfully.

'In the twenty-seventh year, yes.' She smiled brightly, then studied my face and added in a serious tone, 'If your strength does not fail . . . Between that time and this, beloved,' she explained, 'our joys will increase, but so too will our dangers. The more we are given, the more Hecate is angered. And the more she envies us, the more she will assault you to give us both great pain. She will grow ever more frantic and more dangerous in these years approaching your Moment of Passage.'

'I'll take great care,' I assured her. 'Have no fear, I'll be safe.'

Selene smiled at me, pleased by my firm tone. 'You speak to me now,' she observed, 'with the words of strength I spoke to you the first October.'

'Yes,' I laughed, embracing her.

'You will need this greater strength. You must draw upon it soon,' she said in an almost melancholy tone. 'But come now,' she added, 'and let us celebrate this gift with rare foods I have created for your pleasure.'

As we dined at the coffee table, seated on cushions on the floor, I often glanced at the four candles. Observing me, Selene said, 'These signify more than to mark the nights of our love.'

'What?' I asked in surprise.

'They serve also to augment my strength.'

I was amazed by this new revelation. 'I don't understand,' I said stammering. 'Your strength? But it never —'

She stopped me with a warm hand on my shoulder. 'In my world, forever am I strong, unchanging. But in this mortal world,' she explained, a slight sadness in her large dark eyes, 'it is not the same.' She clasped her hands, studying the strong slender fingers silently for a moment.

'My choice of this incarnation in your world meant more restrictions than I have yet explained to you. Your heart senses it. Soon your conscious self will see it. My strength in your world is bound by the cycle of your moon.' She smiled up at me with sweet sadness. 'Do you remember when I came to you at your brother Warren's home, after Hecate brewed the storm Hazel? Was I not then diminished in strength, even as your moon was? A mere shadow of myself?'

'Yes,' I admitted. 'But I heard you, saw you.'

'Only because the power of your faith assisted me, my beloved.'

'But *here,* in our earthly home, my love, you are always the same. Always strong!' I asserted, gripping her arm. 'This arm hasn't changed. It's as firm as always! I can't feel, I can't see, any weakness in it.'

She caressed my hand as it rested on her arm. 'In time you will, beloved Josephine. Soon you will see and feel that this incarnated form is not quite so strong the fourth reunion night as the night before, nor the night when your moon is at its fullest.'

She released my hand and studied my eyes. 'These diminishings are to mortal eyes unseen, to mortal hands unfelt. Yet they are so.'

She paused, swept back her long blonde hair, smiling at me lovingly. 'You approach now your last quarter of your cycle of transformation, Josephine,' she explained. 'You will see more now with your immortal eyes as your self approaches its maturity, less with the imperfect mortal eyes. The longer our reunion periods grow, the clearer will be these diminishings of my strength, linked to the weakening of your moon.'

'I don't care!' I blurted, rising to my feet. 'Very soon we'll be in *your* world. And there won't be these ... these stupid rules,' I added somewhat peevishly.

Selene rose and stared at me sternly. 'Take care!' There was anxiety, almost fear, in her voice. She stepped toward me and seized my hands. Her black eyes burned into my soul. 'All could be lost in an instant,' she said urgently. In a calmer tone she added, 'My beloved one, not yet are you safe from Hecate. Not yet is your immortality with me assured.'

She wrapped her arms around me and held me close. 'Never question the restrictions,' she murmured. 'Never defy the wisdom of the Council. Know too that more is meant by this diminishing of my powers than I can yet reveal to you.'

Feeling ashamed and rightfully admonished for my outburst, I pleaded, 'Forgive my impatience.'

'It is a mortal flaw that still clings to you,' she said, 'but soon it will disappear.' She kissed my brow and my eyelids. 'Your immortal self is now in its adolescence,' she added with a smile, 'often a time of disrespect and arrogance.'

I laughed and promised to fight these adolescent faults.

'Accept these temporary diminishings I must undergo,' she said. 'Know too these lessenings of my powers are done in part to test your worthiness.'

'I've survived worse tests,' I muttered, remembering the losses of Larry's parents and your mother, Laura.

'Yes, but guard against this dangerous pride,' she warned again. 'Know too that Hecate is aware of my periods of diminished strength. She will choose these

139

times particularly to assault you with mighty swords and great spears. These last seven years will hold for us great joys, yet also great perils, Josephine.'

How true her prediction was, Laura! An increasingly angry and jealous Hecate chose the time of *her* fullest powers, the dark of the moon, to take your father's life that following summer. She knew she could hurl spears of despair against my breast for half a month before Selene could help me. But I held firmly to my belief, even as I sat there for days in that hospital room in Richmond, helplessly watching my dear brother Warren, your father, fall into Hecate's clutches.

Laura closed her eyes against the memory of that painful time, the hours and days she and Josie had sat beside that hospital bed, watching her father dying. How outwardly calm, how strong Josie had been until the very moment of his death, when something inside her had snapped. Then she had cried out hysterically, cursing and shouting something Laura could not remember. Laura read on:

I knew your father must die. I knew I could not save him, just as I could not save your mother. The energies of humanity's collective belief in Hecate were too strong in that room where he lay comatose. All minds about him were telling him to die. My mind alone told him to live. But my mind was but one small grain of white sand on an enormous black beach. He could not see it, and his sleeping mind was filled with darkness. So too, near the end, was yours.

* * * * *

Laura shivered at these words. In those final hours, yes — she herself had actually wanted him to die. The wish was felt, not thought or spoken. Yet it was there. She had wanted his suffering to end. How could Josie have known that secret feeling? She read on:

Perhaps you remember an outburst from me at the instant he died. Hecate appeared before me in a waking nightmare vision. I felt her evil self, a shapeless form of darkness and black ice, reach out and seize your father's self from out of his mortal shell. And I heard her hideous, taunting laugh of triumph. And in my grief and my anger at her, I cursed Hecate aloud. I know you must have thought me momentarily mad.

Laura remembered now. Josie had chanted "Damn you, Hecate!" many times, had seemed to be speaking to some invisible presence. Oh Josie, Laura thought sorrowfully, why did I not see your sickness then? She read on:

Three years after this, in August of 1979, began yet another great assault from Hecate, this time directed at my outer shell. You flew from California as soon as you could, shortly after my operation. And for over a week you came to see me every day there at Norfolk General Hospital.

Larry was away, somewhere in South America. You stayed with Debbie and the children, who were living then

141

across the bay, in Hampton. And every day you braved the bridge-tunnel traffic, back and forth across Hampton Roads, to be with me. Sometimes Debbie came too, but not as often, because of the children.

Hecate was truly diabolical, most cunning in this great assault! Not only was the surgery at the dark of the moon, but it was also just six weeks before the time of the October reunion. And shortly after my operation, she hurled Hurricane David across the Outer Banks and up the coast and bay, sweeping all of the Tidewater area. You may imagine my thoughts as I lay there in that hospital bed, hooked up to all that machinery and watching the wind-driven rain beat against my window. But the storm had more sound that substance. Although Hecate frightened everyone, she failed to take any lives. And she altogether failed in her attempt to harm our cottage.

Still she meant to prevent my reunion with Selene. Both you and Debbie helped me in this great battle. You especially helped, Laura, and the doctors and nurses — because you believed, as I did, that I would not die. The power of Hecate was always present in that hospital, as it is in all hospitals, but in my room it was never very strong. All minds in that room held to the light and scorned the darkness. Though Selene was diminished and could not come to me until September 6th, my faith was powerful now, for my immortal self was very near to reaching its full maturity. I knew for certain Selene and I would triumph over Hecate.

But you and Debbie were at times such a hindrance! Though of course, neither of you knew that. Nor could I tell you. But you will understand now what I mean. Both of you fought me tooth and nail over the matter of my going home, remember? The day before you had to fly

142

back to California, September 7th, I told you I meant to go directly to my cottage as soon as I was released from the hospital.

'You are absolutely insane!' you said. 'You will do no such thing! You've already telephoned the sheriff's office. You know there was no damage at all to your house.' You folded your arms, Laura, in that stubborn pose I think you learned from me. 'It's all settled,' you continued. 'You're going to stay in Hampton for a good long while, with Debbie and the kids.'

'Once I'm out of here,' I grumbled at you, 'I'm not going to get into bed again, except to go to sleep.' I practically glared at you. 'My legs are fine,' I added firmly. 'I can still outwalk you.'

You softened somewhat under these reminders of my strength. 'I didn't mean you'd be bedridden,' you said. 'The house is just a few blocks back from the Chesapeake Bay, Josie. You can take walks along the bay.' You smiled, coaxing me.

'Well . . . I'd rather walk on my own beach, where there aren't all those people,' I replied. 'But I guess it won't hurt to stay for a while . . . for a few days.'

Oh I know I seemed to you just a crotchety old woman then, Laura. But what could I do? I couldn't tell you the truth — that the surgery had damaged my self no more than the hurricane had harmed the house. I couldn't tell you then that Selene and I had triumphed over Hecate. Nor that just the previous night Selene had been with me, there in that very room, at the moon's fullness. If I had told you these truths I am telling you now, you and Debbie would have carried me off to Eastern State Hospital, and locked me up in a padded cell in that mental hospital in Williamsburg!

* * * * *

So true, Laura thought. She was glad she had not known then about Josie's psychosis. She was glad Josie had lived her last years in tranquility with her imagined goddess, and not spent them in a hospital for the insane. She read on:

Laura, you meant well, of course, and so did Debbie. So did the doctors, whose opinions I did respect, since they were my allies in this great battle with Hecate, though they didn't know it. But in the end it was Selene's advice I followed, as always. Selene came to me in my sleeping life that very night, granted a second September visitation by the Council.

'They know it is wise that I should be with you for a longer time this month,' she explained as I greeted her with surprise.

'How much longer?' I asked, happily wrapping my arms around her.

'This night and the next. Then you must be without me until our October reunion. But now,' she added brightly, 'you are very strong! Fear not, my beloved. Hecate has retreated in defeat. Even now she lies growling in her den, licking her wounds.'

I laughed with delight and hugged my beloved. Then I told her about your recent visit. I sighed. 'I don't really want to go to Larry and Debbie's home,' I said.

She smiled and nodded. 'I know,' she said gently. 'But it is wise that you go there. Still must you appear as all mortals, Hecate's slave. Subject to decay and death.'

144

I sighed again, but nodded in agreement. 'The illusionary shell is necessary, yes,' I reminded myself aloud.

'Crucial still to our success,' she said, kissing my forehead. 'Go then with Deborah. Let her believe that she nurses you back to health.'

Once Debbie got me into that house in Hampton, she set out to keep me there much longer than I intended to stay. For a while I humored her and played the invalid. But after about a week of this, I realized I had better demonstrate some of my real strength if I hoped to escape in time for the October reunion.

I got up before dawn on a Sunday, quietly left the house, and took a nice long walk, down to the bay and all up and down a long stretch of Chesapeake Avenue. Oh how wonderful it was to watch the sun rising on the bay! Only a few joggers disturbed my solitude. For a while I sat on a grassy bank near the remnants of a short pier and watched a small flock of cormorants diving for fish and then perching on the cockeyed pilings and spreading their black wings to dry them. It was a lovely picture as they stretched and twisted their long thin necks against the mutating colors of the rising sun and the rippling red-golden waters of the bay.

Finally I returned to Debbie's, and started a load of laundry — my things, mostly. Then I began vacuuming the living room.

'What on earth do you think you're doing?' Debbie shouted as she came thundering down the stairs in her bathrobe, her bleached hair bouncing wildly. 'You can't do that!' She unplugged the machine and stared at me, amazement and fear flashing in her green eyes.

'I am doing it,' I replied calmly.

She plopped down on the couch, gazing at me open-mouthed. 'Honestly, Josie,' she stammered, 'you mustn't —'

I told her about my long walk. 'I don't believe it!' she exclaimed. 'By yourself? Three hours ago? What if you had gotten dizzy, fallen? Dr. Hertzler will absolutely —'

I interrupted, 'The sunrise was gorgeous on the bay. You really ought to get up and watch it sometime!'

That Friday, September 21st, young Dr. Hertzler took out my stitches. Debbie of course accompanied me to his office. I asked him then if I could go home soon.

'The middle of nowhere!' Debbie protested. 'She lives by herself, Dr. Hertzler. She shouldn't be out there by herself yet.'

He folded his glasses and put them into the pocket of his white jacket. Then he said, 'Miss Westmoreland, you've had major surgery.'

I said somewhat peevishly, 'But you got all of it, the cancer. And I feel fine. I'm walking five miles a day now.' At the word *cancer*, I noticed, Debbie tensed and looked pained. Oh yes, I thought, Hecate does frighten mortals mightily with this weapon. Even young Hertzler looked slightly uncomfortable — ever so slightly, but I detected it in the awkward way he touched his little brown beard.

Hertzler cleared his throat and smiled. 'Yes,' he said, nodding, 'I think we did get it all. But there are no guarantees in medicine, you know. I'll want to keep a close eye on you for some time yet, Miss Westmoreland. I'll want to see you weekly for a while, less than that later.'

'That's no problem,' I assured him. 'I can drive up here in about two hours' time. Just give me a list of the appointments.'

146

Debbie interposed anxiously, 'She needs to stay right here in the area for at least a month more, don't you think?'

Hertzler looked from her to me. 'Can you get somebody to stay with your for a while on Hatteras?'

'Oh yes!' I exclaimed. 'Week after next, yes.'

'Who?' Debbie asked suspiciously.

'A good friend,' I said to her. 'She'll be there for almost a whole week. She comes every fall,' I added.

'Who is she?' Debbie asked, frowning slightly.

'Somebody you don't know. She's an old friend. A longtime friend,' I corrected myself. 'She's younger than you.' I glanced at Debbie's somewhat plump body. 'And in better shape than you,' I added. 'In perfect health, that is.'

Debbie reddened slightly. 'Does Laura know this friend?'

'No, Laura doesn't know her,' I grumbled, growing irritated by this interrogation.

Dr. Hertzler intervened at this point. 'Miss Westmoreland, if I'm as satisfied next Friday as I am now, I'll let you go back home soon. Back to Hatteras. When will your friend be there?'

I pulled my pocket calendar from my purse. 'October the third. Wednesday.'

Hertzler smiled at me. 'And you just might be there to greet her,' he said.

Debbie threw up her hands. 'I don't approve of this. I don't approve of it at all!' She looked at the young doctor coldly.

I pulled the white sheet around me and quickly got down from the examination table, beaming at Hertzler. At the door he paused and said to Debbie, loud enough for me to hear, 'She's a remarkable woman. She's got the vital signs of a woman half her age. Rarely have I had a patient her age heal so rapidly. You don't need to worry, Mrs. Westmoreland. Another week of your fine care and she should be ready to leave. I'll not let her go if I have any doubts at all.' Looking past Debbie briefly, he winked at me and smiled.

I humored Debbie by letting her drive me to Hatteras in her Buick. Her nephew Bobby took a holiday from high school and followed us down in my station wagon. We got to the cottage around ten that morning, October 3, 1979. It was a warm, summer-like day. I sat patiently rocking on the porch while Debbie unpacked my clothes and Bobby opened the storm shutters and swept sand off the porch. I was bursting with joy, knowing that soon I could stop playing the invalid, and soon too, at twilight, I would again be in Selene's arms.

Debbie asked anxiously, 'What if Mabel doesn't get here tonight? Or gets here late?'

I smiled. 'Oh she'll be here all right. And right on time.' I yawned, somewhat drowsy after the drive down in the too-comfortable Buick. 'She's never been late yet . . . not for twenty-four years.'

'I thought you said Mabel's about my age,' Debbie said.

'Younger.' I yawned again.

'You said twenty-four years just now.'

'No, a little older than that. She's about thirty.'

Debbie frowned and shook her head. 'No, I mean you said she's never been late for twenty-four years.'

I realized I had slipped. I reddened slightly and chuckled. 'I meant "for years." She's not been late for years,' I explained.

'Oh.'

I saw that suspicious look on her face again. I got her out of the cottage and back to Hampton, but not soon enough to suit me. She insisted on making my bed, tidying up, and forcing a too-rich lunch on me before she left, at about two o'clock.

A brisk walk on the beach helped burn up the lunch, but I was still drowsy afterwards. At about three-thirty I went to bed for a short nap, but fell into a deep sleep.

At twilight I was gently awakened by a soft kiss on my lips from my beloved Selene. How wonderful to open my eyes and see her incarnated radiance bent over me! She gently unbuttoned my blouse, then softly kissed each breast. Yes, of course *both* of them were there, for it was my self she embraced now, not the damaged body.

I laughed and pulled her onto me. 'What will Hecate try next?' I asked. 'To take a leg or an arm?'

We discussed again why Hecate had thus assaulted my mortal shell. 'She has no understanding of love,' Selene said. 'But she has seen how, among mortals, love often dies after a bodily loss such as this. And she knows such a loss is one most dreaded by mortal women.'

'She foolishly hoped, by this, you would stop loving me,' I commented.

'Or that you would fall into her web of self-doubt and despair.' She smiled, stroking my face.

'She lives in total ignorance,' I observed.

'She is the darkness, yes. So in her darkness she lives.'

'The darkness of ignorance,' I added, deep in thought. 'And this then is why, though I have often felt her presence, often seen her power in this world, never have I *seen* Hecate, as I see you.' I touched Selene's smooth, soft face, smiled into her dark bright eyes. 'She *has* no face!' I declared. 'She cannot be touched like this.'

'Never!' Selene said. 'For she is a void, merely the absence of light, of truth, of understanding. Therefore she dwells in veiled mists, false dreams, nightmare

149

visions . . . mere illusions. The imaginations of misguided mortals. Light destroys her substance, reveals that she is not real.'

'And yet she rules this mortal world,' I said with a sigh. 'The collective mortal mind has been enslaved by this, its own fiendish creation.' I sat silently pondering these truths about Hecate for some time.

Then I remembered my promise to Debbie that I would drive to Rodanthe and call her as soon as 'Mabel' arrived, to put her mind at ease. I chuckled and explained to Selene my recent trials with overly anxious Debbie. 'You have yet another name now among mortals,' I said with a laugh. 'Mabel!'

I kept the telephone call short. Debbie was not entirely mollified when she learned I had driven alone to the phone booth. She had hoped to meet 'Mabel' over the telephone. 'She's cooking supper for us,' I said. 'I had a long nap this afternoon, and I feel fine. I feel truly like myself again, now that I'm home.' I smiled to myself, promised to call again on the weekend, and hung up.

Debbie's curiosity might have become a serious problem eventually. But fortunately, soon after this, Larry was transferred to Germany. I can't tell you how relieved I was that he took the family with him.

This was the twenty-fifth year, 1979. By now the Council had extended our October reunion time to five nights, which is why Selene had arrived this October on the third, two nights before the total fullness of the moon.

On the night of the absolute fullness, as we sat dining on delicacies, Selene said, 'In this recent great assault, Hecate used even those you love against you in her attempt to possess you and thus bring misery to us both.'

I nodded. 'She even used Laura.'

'Your favorite relative,' she commented.

150

'Oh yes!' I exclaimed. I love them all, but Laura is the one I find dearest. I *like* her the most.' I paused, then added, 'Maybe because she is most like me.'

Selene smiled. 'I have happy news about Laura.'

I looked at her eagerly. 'What happy news? And please don't tease me,' I pleaded.

'No, I will not demand you be patient,' she said with a laugh. 'This gift I may reveal to you now. This latest victory over Hecate has pleased the Council most greatly. The reward is —' She paused and took my hands. 'A gift for Laura! The Council has granted that the story of our love be told to her.'

I jumped to my feet with joy! I shouted gleefully, 'I can tell Laura? Tell her all?'

Selene laughed and nodded. 'Yes, my beloved. But not quite all. And not with spoken words.'

'Then what —'

'Much of what you have written of our love, in your private journals,' she explained, 'you may leave behind, for Laura to read — after the Moment of Passage. But she must not know these truths until then! The veil cannot be lifted for her until after our Year of Eternity begins.'

I nodded enthusiastically. 'Yes, yes,' I agreed. 'This is most wise.'

'And she may not know all. The mortal mind cannot endure the full light, as you know.' She explained how, from that time until the Moment of Passage, each month she would guide me through my journals. And from these we would prepare together this record of what you, dear niece, would be allowed to know.

So excited was I over the news of this most marvelous gift to you that I danced about like a child at Christmas. 'Oh, I can hardly wait to start!' I exclaimed. 'I wonder if

151

my old typewriter . . . Well, I can get if fixed. Such a marvelous, truly wonderful gift for Laura!'

She smiled and embraced me warmly. 'A well-earned gift, my beloved.'

'And all the details *must* be perfect,' I continued, waving my arms and pacing. 'The account *must* be absolutely accurate.'

'See how strong now your self has grown,' she said with approval. 'You now seek perfection in all things, as we Immortals always do.'

On our last night together at that Silver Anniversary time, as Selene stood lighting the five tall candles at our windows, I detected in her face a paleness I had never seen before. Somewhat startled, I moved quickly to her side and put my arm around her shoulders. 'You appear to me weakened,' I said with concern and some confusion. 'Surely Hecate cannot touch you.'

She smiled at me with effort and took my arm. 'It is not Hecate,' she said softly, 'no. Have you forgotten the diminishing I spoke of, in our twenty-first October?' As I led her toward the couch, she added, 'Before, you could not consciously perceive it. But now that your immortal self nears the moment of full maturity, you must see more of it, and see it now more clearly, each reunion time.'

'I don't fully understand it,' I said with a sigh, tucking an afghan around her legs. 'This restriction of your powers seems arbitrary to me.'

Selene pulled me to her side on the couch. I felt at that instant a deep glow within my self, and then an upward surging I cannot fully explain in words. Many times before I had felt it when she embraced me, and I can liken it only to an orgasmic surge. It was this a hundredfold, and yet something more. How can I explain it? It was like — an overwhelming surge of the purest energy. The distilled essence, if you can imagine this, Laura, of all that mortals call life.

Gently Selene withdrew her arm from me. Breathing heavily, I dropped my head weakly against her shoulder, every fiber of my being still vibrating from this rapture. And then slowly calming, like the stilled strings of a violin laid aside by its player. Slipping into a blissful afterglow like sleep, I heard her softly whisper to me, 'To strengthen your immortal self, sometimes I must give to you my own immortality.'

I write to you, dearest niece, in the Year of Eternity, the twenty-eighth year of our earthly love. This mortal shell is now seventy earth years of age. Mortals see me as an old woman. But I am a fresh young adult in my eternal substance. And filled with great joy and a peace beyond all description!

The Immortal Council's last, and most gracious, gift to Selene and me has been to grant us fourteen October nights together at our earthly home. These have dated from the total blackness of the earth's moon to the complete fullness of it, to occur quite soon — October 3, 1982, by this planet's calendar.

It is now the first evening of October. Selene and I together are preparing for my Moment of Passage. And I am typing for you this final chapter of our story. It lies in your own power, Laura, to keep this true account secret, or to share it with other mortals. Like all mortals, you are free to choose your own destiny, free to learn from, or to ignore, these revelations the Council has permitted me to record for you.

I may not tell you where the Place of the Immortals exists. I may tell you only that though it is far from the galaxy of this earth, it is not beyond the reach of humankind. In centuries to come, your mortal world might find it. But not until Hecate's powers have greatly diminished in your world.

The Council, and my beloved Selene also, wish me to reveal to you too that your earth lives in a darkness of its own making — sadly so, unnecessarily so. It lives servile to the powers of the false Hecate, whose powers are sustained only by the mortal flaws of fear and despair. If mortals would cling to the light and deny her illusionary darkness, they could transform this planet into a second Place of the Immortals.

This much also I may reveal to you: I am not the first mortal chosen to receive this gift of Eternity, nor will I be the last. The imperfectly understood records of your earth's ancients who glimpsed the fuller light will bear witness to this fact. Read again, dear niece, the records of the ancient Greeks and Romans. And read too, with a deeper understanding, the Bible that has been so badly mangled by our forefathers. Many others on this planet have been tested. Many others will be. Though most mortals have failed to achieve the Moment of Passage, some few have succeeded. And in future eons, perhaps many more will succeed.

This much am I permitted to tell you about the Moment of Passage: for no two chosen mortals is the earth time, nor the earth place, nor the earth manner for this passage the same. For each chosen one, there are individual paths, though these are similar.

For me, the place of the Moment of Passage is to be the shore of the Atlantic Ocean, directly before this cottage Selene and I have shared as our earthly home for twenty-eight of your earth years. There I will first perform certain sacred rites. The time of my Passage will be during the absolute fullness of the earth's moon, two nights from now — the third of October.

At this appointed time, Selene will take me with her to the Place of the Immortals. I will undergo at this moment my final test of faith. We will join hands, then step together upon the silver path that lies across the waves of the sea. I know I will not turn back in fear of the waters! I know I will firmly hold the hand of my beloved. Together we will cross, unharmed, the waters that once, in my mortal form, I feared. Together we will cross this silver path of light, and walk into our Eternity!

CHAPTER SIX
Sunday, 6:00 P.M., October 10

As always, Tate was polite. "Evening, Miz Westmoreland," he said, smiling and removing his officer's cap. "I hope this ain't an inconvenient time for you. I reckon you got my —"

"Yes," Laura interrupted. "I got the note. Thank you. And please come in." Her tone was flat, almost emotionless. Tate's brow furrowed slightly. He followed her silently down the hallway into the living room.

She motioned toward the chair. He unzipped his jacket and sat down, loosening his necktie and studying her face. He rubbed his chin slowly and then asked, "Miz Westmoreland, are you all right, ma'am?"

She saw concern in his pale blue eyes and smiled at him somewhat weakly. "Well, yes," she said reassuringly, "but — " She broke off, nervously running her hand through her hair. Then with a little laugh she said, "It's a long story. A very long story." Then she added, "It calls for a glass of wine, in fact." Without waiting for his response she left for the kitchen.

After she returned and poured the wine, Laura pointed to the blue notebook lying on the coffee table. "Josie left this behind," she said. "I just finished reading it a few minutes ago."

"Oh?" He hunched forward, looking down at it.

Laura sat down on the couch. She explained how she had been led to Josie's hidden notebook.

He looked at the cover and the title page, then looked up at Laura. "Some kind of autobiography?" he asked.

She nodded. "Yes. Written for me . . . but you'll have to read it too." Her composure broke. "Oh damn," she said softly. She stood and began pacing the floor. He watched her, his brow furrowed, a big weathered hand slowly rubbing his stubbled chin.

She sighed, sat back down. "You were so right," she said, almost in a whisper. She picked up the wine glass and continued, meeting his eyes and speaking more firmly, "She did drown. And right here. Right out there!" She gestured toward the windows behind him. She quickly drank some wine.

"I am sorry, ma'am," Tate said gently. "I truly —"

"She walked right out into that ocean!" Laura almost shouted the words, the full impact of what she had just read hitting her now like an electrical shock. "All her life terrified of death by drowning," she continued, her voice almost breaking, "and yet —" She broke off, sobbing softly.

She took the handkerchief Tate offered, wiped her eyes. He waited silently while she regained her composure. When he pulled his cigarettes from the pocket of his shirt, she asked for one. As he lit it for her, he said, "I didn't think you smoked, ma'am."

"I don't," she said. Something in his puzzled expression made her laugh briefly, releasing some of her grief.

He smiled, momentarily touched her shoulder in a gesture of sympathy, then leaned back, waiting.

"I'm okay now," she said, folding the handkerchief and returning it to him.

He coughed, cleared his throat. In a gentle tone he asked, tapping the closed notebook, "Now let me get this straight, Miz Westmoreland, about this story here." He paused, seeming to weigh each word carefully. "Are you saying that your aunt wrote to you, right here, that she meant to commit suicide, that she intended to drown herself in the Atlantic?"

Laura smiled sadly, remembering Josie's description of the silver path across the waves, the hand-in-hand walk above the black waters with Selene to the Place of the Immortals. "No," she answered softly, "that's not what she meant. It's complex. Very complex."

The two light blue letters fell out of the notebook as Tate leaned forward to replace it on the coffee table. He glanced at Laura with raised eyebrows as he picked them up from the floor.

"Read those first," Laura said. "She wrote them on the day she died. Last Sunday." Tate tucked them into the manuscript. "And then read her story. Some of it is very personal." She smiled to herself, remembering the love scenes. How these at first had surprised, then moved her, then finally helped her to acknowledge and then embrace her own feelings, that part of herself she had denied for so many years.

She rested a hand lightly, almost fondly, on the blue cover, sad that Josie was dead, but happy that her life had been joyful. She looked up at Tate. "There are certain... intimate details here," she said. She caught his slightly startled look, and remembered her own initial reaction to the discovery that the outwardly reserved, reclusive Josie had been a woman of deep passion. She smiled at Tate. "Some parts might even shock you."

His face flushed slightly; he shifted in his seat. "Yes, ma'am." He cleared his throat.

"Don't skip a single word," Laura said firmly, handing him the notebook. "All of it is crucial. It explains everything," she added, remembering the words of Josie's letter. "The path of circles she drew in the sand, the painting in her bedroom, the reason she . . . died as she did." Laura crushed out the half-smoked cigarette.

At the back door he thanked her for giving him the notebook. "It's material evidence, ma'am. I appreciate that you chose not to suppress it."

She smiled weakly. "How could I? You asked me to help you find out what happened to Josie, didn't you?"

She fixed a simple dinner of fruit and canned soup. By eight o'clock she was driving the rented Mustang south down Route 12.

The rusting sign nailed near the door proclaimed the general store open on Sundays till 9:00 p.m.

Hand-lettered signs inside the windows read BLOODWORMS MINNOWS BEACHWEAR 50% OFF. The dimly lighted metal strip along the eaves below the weathered shingled roof announced, in fading letters: BEER BAIT ICE BREAD MILK. And at each end of it, plate-shaped, the old Coca-Cola logo.

Only the proprietor was inside — a stocky, red-faced, middle-aged man who eyed Laura curiously, then returned to his task of applying price stickers to cans of Dinty Moore Beef Stew.

Like the wood-shingled store, the single telephone booth seemed to have been there since the 1930s. The sturdy wood of it was blackened; the hinged glass door squeaked loudly. The built-in corner seat was well-worn; the inside walls carved with initials, scratched with phone numbers.

Laura's hand trembled as she lifted the receiver. Would Jackie even be there on a Sunday afternoon? What should she say to her first? Would Jackie even listen?

Jackie's number rang once, twice, a third time.

"Hello?" It was a woman's voice, but not Jackie's.

Laura felt a ringing sensation in her ears. "Uh, hello," she stammered, swallowing. "Is, uh, Jackie there?"

"Yes. Who's calling, please?" the woman asked.

"Uh, Laura. Laura Westmoreland."

"Hold on, please."

Laura combed her fingers nervously through her hair. She could hear the woman calling out to Jackie, a dog barking in the background. Was it too late? Was this woman Jackie's lover?

"Laura?"

For a moment Laura could not answer, and then words rushed out of her. "Oh Jackie, I'm so sorry," she

160

said, her voice breaking, "and I've been such a *fool* and I don't know what to say —" She broke off, choking back the sobs rising in her chest.

"Where are you? Let me come over there to talk. My sister's here right now. Marty, the one from Kansas City."

Laughing through her sobs, Laura answered, "Come over here? Oh God, how I wish you could . . . But I'm in North Carolina."

"What?"

"The Outer Banks of North Carolina." She wiped her eyes, regaining her composure somewhat. Then Laura said, again choking back tears, "I'm here because — Josie's dead, Jackie." The grief flooded back through her now that she was speaking this fact to someone she loved.

"I'm sorry, Laura," Jackie said softly. There was all the concern, the warmth, the gentleness that Laura remembered. "Do you want to tell me about it?"

"Last Sunday, a week ago. And then the sheriff called me, on Wednesday, and I flew out. She was just missing then, you see — No, she was already dead, but —" She broke off in tears.

"Laura, Laura, it's all right, Laura," Jackie said, her voice soothing, reassuring. "You don't have to talk now, sweetheart. It's all right."

"And I'm so sorry, too . . . I want you to know that."

"I know you are," Jackie said sympathetically. "I know you loved her very much."

The laugh rose involuntarily. "You wonderful, crazy — I meant you, Jackie." She paused. "I've accepted it, Josie's death. I was trying to tell you — I guess I'm not making much sense, am I?"

"Listen, is there anybody with you? Your cousin?"

161

"No. Larry and Debbie are still in Germany." She wiped her eyes. She felt calmer now. "But I'm okay, really."

"Listen," Jackie said, "I've got to get Marty to the airport. She's flying back this afternoon. Give me the number there and let me call you back in a few hours."

"You can't call me back. There's no phone at Josie's house. I'm in a phone booth." Through the glass doors of the booth she saw the stocky proprietor of the store, arms folded across his thick chest, staring in her direction as he leaned back against the counter. "This store I'm in — remember *The Waltons?* Ike's store? It's like that. And the man closes up at nine."

"You're kidding. That's the only place with a telephone?"

"Well I could try the village of Hatteras — that's about thirty or forty miles south. Or Nags Head, north of the island —"

"No, no, sweetheart," Jackie interrupted. "Don't drive around like that trying to find a telephone booth tonight."

"But I do want to — And he's ready to close up here."

"Listen, Laura, you've been through a lot," Jackie said gently. "Why don't you just go back to your aunt's place, try to get some sleep. And then phone me tomorrow when Ike opens his store again." Laura could almost hear the smile, see the grin. Jackie continued, "I've got the day off tomorrow. You can phone anytime at all. I'll be here all day. Just me and crazy West."

Laura felt her eyes moistening. The love, the caring — it was still there. She heard it, felt it. "Oh Jackie," she whispered, "I am so sorry, so sorry for . . . my horrible, stupid words to you."

162

"It's okay," Jackie said softly. "Don't think about it now. Just get some rest."

Laura sniffed and laughed softly. "I've not really even asked you properly," she said. "And you've already forgiven me, haven't you?"

"Yes. A long time ago."

The stocky storekeeper rapped lightly on the glass and pointed to his watch. Laura nodded and he walked away. "I've, uh, just been notified by our friend Ike the owner that I've got to hang up. There's so much more I want to say, but —"

"It's okay, sweetheart." In the distance Laura heard a bark from the dog Jackie had named after her.

"Give West a hug for me," she said. "I miss her."

"She misses you too. And so do I," Jackie said softly.

"Maybe I don't even have the right to say it now," Laura said, "but . . . I love you, Jackie."

"I love you too," Jackie said in an almost hoarse whisper. "Call me tomorrow, collect. Anytime. Goodnight now, darling."

Laura smiled, wiping her eyes as she hung up. As she walked quickly across the wooden floor toward the door of the general store, she smiled cheerfully at the stocky owner and said, "Goodnight, Ike. And thank you!" He stared, frowned slightly and nodded as she passed. As she strode briskly through the doorway she heard him mumble, "Tourists."

CHAPTER SEVEN
Monday, October 11, 1982

"What's this?" Laura asked as Tate stepped inside, extending a foil-wrapped package.

"Oh, just a little something my wife sent over." He smiled, removing his cap. "Hope you like pecan pie."

"Oh indeed I do!" She grinned, accepting the package. "This is awfully nice of her. Please do thank her for me."

Tate followed her into the kitchen. He placed Josie's manuscript near the oil lamp burning on the round oak table.

"Have a seat," Laura said, moving toward the kerosene stove. "I'm fixing some coffee for us. I played tourist a little today. I drove up to Nags Head." She turned and smiled at him. "Tomorrow these legs of mine are going to remember what I put them through climbing Jockey's Ridge again, after six years."

Tate chuckled and shook his head. "Been a long time since I last did that. That's a whole lot of sand to wade through."

"Oh but the view at the top!" she exclaimed. "I could see all the way south to the bridge. And north," she added, "to the monument."

"Yes, ma'am, it is a lovely sight from there, on a clear day like today was." He smiled to himself. "When I was a boy, I used to think to myself, looking down from that crest there, that it was like I was a seagull. Seeing all of it, you know. The ocean, and Roanoke Sound, and all the land for miles. So then, you had a nice day, ma'am?"

"Yes indeed. Very nice."

"And I reckon then you're feeling a whole lot better about things?" He studied her.

"Much better, yes." She nodded. "A hundred percent better, in fact." She smiled to herself, remembering the major highlight of her day: the two-hour telephone talk with Jackie.

"It's so complex," she had said to Jackie. "I still haven't sorted it all out. It's going to take a while, Jackie, to explain it to you. And to myself. I said I couldn't love you because I couldn't say I didn't love you, and I was

165

afraid to say I did! Oh I'm not making any sense at all, am I?"

She could almost see the coast-to-coast grin when Jackie chuckled. "Well, some, sweetheart," Jackie answered. "But don't worry about it right now. Just finish what you have to do there . . . and then come home, darling." Laura would never forget what Jackie had said just after that: "We've got a lifetime, now, to talk it over."

Tate declined Laura's offer of a slice of the pecan pie, patting his stomach and declaring himself "full as a tick on a bloodhound."

She glanced at the closed notebook on the table. "Well," she began, "I guess you've read all of it."

He coughed. "Yes ma'am. Every word." He toyed with the large shell she'd placed near him for an ashtray. "Didn't feel quite comfortable reading the real personal parts —" He broke off with a nervous laugh, reddening slightly. "Sort of felt like a peeping Tom, you know. But like you told me, this story here is indeed very important." He lit a cigarette and offered Laura one. She shook her head no.

"It's kinda ironic, you know, the title she put on it," he continued. "Her *True Story*."

Laura nodded. "And yet, in a way, it *is* true. It *does* explain everything, as Josie said it would."

Tate stared thoughtfully at his coffee mug. "What she wrote there about immortality and all," he said, shaking his head slowly, "that was very strange, a real sad delusion she had . . . But you know, a lotta what she said was real, too. Very true facts. The part about Hurricane Hazel, for instance. I was about fifteen when Hazel hit here. She's right about the date, the evacuations of the islands. Just everything." He sipped his coffee and looked up at Laura. "In fact, she's got the dates right, ma'am,

about all the other hurricanes she talked about there."
He looked at Laura quizzically. "That's kinda strange,
don't you think? Mixing up the real and the unreal like
that?"

A prose passage from *Hamlet* came to Laura's mind: *I
am but mad north-north-west: when the wind is southerly
I know a hawk from a handsaw.* She said to Tate, "Mental
illness can be complex. The psychotic person is often very
acute, very rational in most respects." She sighed and ran
a hand through her hair. "Even close relatives don't
always see the illness. I never saw it in Josie . . . not at
all."

"Well, ma'am," he said gently, "you shouldn't feel
bad about that. You didn't see her much those last years."

Laura smiled at him. "Oh I don't feel bad about it —
not now."

"Looks to me like she had a pretty happy life," he
commented, "even if a lot of it wasn't real. I guess the
parts about your family were true though, weren't they?"

"Oh yes. The deaths, her cancer operation." She
smiled, remembering the scenes in Norfolk and Hampton
with Josie, Debbie, and herself. "She described our family
most accurately."

Tate pushed back the oak chair and rose from the
kitchen table, carrying his mug. "One other funny thing,"
he commented, "was how right she was about the moon.
Mind if I warm this, ma'am?"

"Go right ahead."

"Every blessed time she said the moon was full," he
continued, "or half-full, or whatever — she was
absolutely right."

"Really? How do you know?" she asked with interest.

He walked back to the table and sat down. "Well, my
wife, you see — Dorothy — she's a regular pack rat. Never

167

throws out anything. Up in our attic she's got a big old cardboard box fulla calendars, going back to the fifties. Don't know why she keeps 'em, but she does. Anyhow, I got kinda curious about those dates your aunt kept giving there. So I got down that old box of calendars and checked 'em out." He pulled his little notebook from his pocket and showed Laura the list of dates and his checkmarks. "Right on target," he said, "year after year and month after month, for twenty-eight years." He looked at Laura. "Ain't that something?"

She shivered slightly at the strangeness of this accuracy. "Yes, it is . . . unusual. But as I said before," she continued in a somewhat professional tone, "cases of psychosis can be quite complex." And this one, she now realized, was amazing and unique. She grasped for an explanation. "What Josie wrote," she began slowly, "is . . . an account of imagined events, but events that happened — in her psychotic imagination, at actual times." She leaned back in her chair and folded her arms. "A classic case of psychosis," she added.

"I see," he said, looking at her with respect. "Psychosis, huh?"

"Basically, an inability to distinguish between what's real and what's imagined. A very serious mental disorder."

"Her death then," he asked, hunching forward, "would you, as a psychologist, call it a suicide?"

"I'd have to say she took her own life . . . but I would not call it suicide."

"Me neither," he said, slapping a heavy hand on the table. "The law defines suicide as the *willful* taking of your own life. And this lady did not *intend* to drown when she walked out into that water out there, did she?"

"No, she didn't," Laura agreed.

He smiled and nodded. For a moment he sat quietly smoking and sipping his coffee. Then he said, "This notebook here, Miz Westmoreland, I think it's gonna help your case more than it'll hurt it. Yes ma'am." He patted the closed manuscript briefly. "In *my* professional opinion, as well as yours, it's material evidence of an accidental drowning." He smiled with self-satisfaction. "The lady did not *mean* to die, did not intend it. I reckoned that much even before I read one word in this notebook. And I'll back you in court, ma'am, all the way, I assure you."

"Well, thank you," Laura said with a smile. "I appreciate that. But I don't think my opinion is going to be admissible."

"No, not since you're the one, mainly, that stands to benefit, you and your cousin. But I reckon your opinion's likely to be backed by that of other folks who can testify, other psychologists."

"Well, not necessarily. Psychologists and psychiatrists don't always agree, you know."

"Yes ma'am, I do know. But you're sure gonna have a lotta testimony on your side. Though you can count on it those insurance people'll put up a fight . . . have their lawyers, and *their* experts swarming all over this story like flies at an outdoor crab picking." He shook his head, looked up at her. "Sad part is, they're gonna make it mighty uncomfortable for you, ma'am. Gonna drag out all this business, you know, about your aunt's, uh, personal —"

"Her homosexuality. Lesbianism."

"Yes ma'am." He cleared his throat, drummed his fingers on the oak table. "And the real shame is, you know, that *that* ain't the point here."

Laura looked at him with some surprise.

169

He continued, his eyes looking not so much at Laura as at some abstract judge, or jury, "The point is, this lady, living all alone, and craving for somebody to love, somebody to share her life with, invented such a person in her mind. And then she believed this person was real, and she got sicker and sicker in her mind over the years, until this idea, this delusion, just took over. And it caused her to die. And *that,*" he added firmly, "is the point. It ain't relevant at all who this imaginary person was, or whether it was a man or a woman."

Laura felt like applauding. She smiled at him with admiration. "You really ought to have been a lawyer, Sheriff Tate. I'd hire you in an instant."

"Oh no, ma'am," he replied, flushing slightly. "I'd be no good at that. I ain't much for public speaking."

"But you certainly do know what justice means. Which is more than can be said of some lawyers I've known about." She reflected for a moment. "You're right of course. Because it was a Greek goddess and not a Greek god that Josie loved, this might get ugly in a courtroom."

"It ain't right that it should," he said, looking at her sympathetically, "but I reckon it probably will, ma'am, yes. I thought I oughtta prepare you for that — the likelihood your opposition's gonna try to make your deceased aunt look, well . . . not like the fine lady she really was."

The thought angered Laura, but then she observed, more to herself than to him, "They can't hurt her now."

"No ma'am," he agreed. "But I hope they won't hurt you, by talking about her like, like . . . something less than human."

"I'll be able to handle it," she said reassuringly, refilling their coffee mugs. "You know, I have the impression that on a personal level you didn't have too

170

much trouble accepting Josie's homosexuality. It really doesn't bother you — not seriously." She looked at him, curious about his response.

"Well," he said, "I'll be honest. I did feel a little bit uncomfortable reading those personal parts. But then again," he added, reddening slightly, "I reckon it would of been just about the same, my feelings, you know, if there'd been a Sam in there in the bed with your aunt instead of another lady. It's just that, well . . . it was kinda private, you know, what I was reading. I sorta felt like it wasn't none of my business, what they did in private."

Laura felt like hugging him. "The world could use a few million more people like you, Sheriff Tate," she said with a grin.

For a moment he stared vacantly past her, apparently lost in his own thoughts. Then, folding his arms and leaning back in his chair he said, "I got this first cousin, you know. Clarence. His daddy and my daddy were brothers. Clarence lives up in Norfolk now. He's a lawyer, in fact. Real good one too, they say." He chuckled. "At least one of us Tates turned out to be a lawyer. Anyway, me and Clarence grew up together out here. Little place near Cape Hatteras called Buxton." He smiled, a faraway look in his eyes. "Oh we had a lotta great times together when we were boys. Together all the time, just like brothers." He paused, seemingly recalling some happy memory.

Then his face darkened slightly. "Well, anyhow . . . In high school, one day this teacher, he found Clarence and this other boy, well . . . kissing, or something. In the boys' locker room at the gym." Tate rubbed his chin, frowning. "Whatever it was, just overnight everything was different."

"The boys were punished," Laura suggested, encouraging his story.

"Punished?" Tate's chuckle was bitter. "Crucified, I'd say. Uncle Walt kicked Clarence out of the house . . . Didn't even talk to him about it, no sir. Sixteen years old, and standing out there on that dirt road with nothing but the clothes on his back." He paused, rubbing his chin, staring past Laura. "He came to our house," Tate continued softly. "And thank God, my daddy let him in. He stayed with me up in my room. And all night long, he just cried and cried."

"It had to be very, very rough," Laura murmured. "But his life's okay now, you said?"

"Yes ma'am, but it wasn't easy for him, no sir. For about a week he stayed with us and kept going to school." Tate shook his head. "But he just couldn't take it — the way people laughed, ganged up to shove him around, wrote things on the bathroom walls about him and the other boy. I couldn't blame him for wanting to leave the island. I woulda felt like that too, I reckon." Tate reached for his pack of cigarettes. "My daddy lent him fifty dollars — about all he could afford, being a waterman with five of us to support — and paid for his bus ticket to Norfolk. And I gave him all the money I'd saved up, less'en ten dollars I reckon."

"With a start in life like that," Laura said, shaking her head in wonderment, "how on earth did he manage to become a lawyer?"

"Pure-T-guts." Laura smiled at the southern phrase. "Stayed at the Y in Norfolk," Tate continued. "Went to school, worked afternoons, nights, weekends doing any kinda work he could get. Then he went up to Williamsburg and worked his way through college, and

172

then law school. Got some scholarships to help him. Made the honor roll, all the time."

"He sounds like an incredible man," Laura remarked. "I guess you kept in touch with him all those years?"

"Yes ma'am! And I still do . . . Reckon I always will, matter of fact." He leaned forward, toyed with his shell ashtray. "He comes down here ever' now and then on vacation. Usually stays up at Nags Head. But we always get together for a little fishing." He looked up at Laura. "We talk about a lotta things, but I don't ask no questions about his private life. He never did get married, but it ain't my business why . . . He's got a friend lives with him up there in Norfolk. Real nice fella. Retired naval officer." Tate smiled to himself. "Clarence thinks a whole lot of him, and that's good enough for me."

Laura grinned. "Clarence sounds like just the lawyer I'm going to be needing here on the east coast, and very soon. Before I leave here I want you to give me his address and telephone number."

She got up to reheat her coffee. "By the way," she said over her shoulder, "whatever happened to the other boy, Clarence's friend in high school?"

"Oh, I'm not really sure," Tate answered. "His folks sent him off somewhere and he never came back to Hatteras. The rumor was they sent him up to Williamsburg, to Eastern State Hospital."

Laura shook her head sadly. "The other response," she said softly. "If you're homosexual, you're either downright wicked or you're crazy."

"I reckon that's about the way most folks see it. But Clarence ain't either one," he added firmly. "That's why I say the romantic part of anybody's life — your aunt's life, too — that ain't never really the point."

173

Again Laura felt like hugging him. Instead she smiled at him with open admiration and insisted he share some of his wife's pecan pie with her. As they were eating, she asked, "Would you do me one favor? Call me Laura."

"Yes ma'am," he answered with a grin. "If you'll call me Bill."

She reached across the table and shook his hand. "I am very happy, Bill Tate, that I've met you."

"Happy to make your acquaintance too, Miz West —" He broke off in a chuckle. "I mean, Laura."

She laughed and asked him to tell her all about his wife, Dorothy, and his children.

CHAPTER EIGHT
Friday, October 21, 1983:
One Year Later

"You weren't exaggerating, darling," Jackie said. "This is totally unlike the California coast." She studied the sandy landscape through her lens, then grinned at Laura, who was driving the rented Pontiac. "Radically different! No rocks, cliffs . . . I haven't seen a tree either, not since we crossed that bridge at, uh —"

"Currituck Sound." Laura smiled at her, pleased with Jackie's enthusiastic interest in the Outer Banks. They had stopped briefly for Jackie to photograph the Wright Brothers Memorial, then Jockey's Ridge. Now they were driving south on N.C. Route 12. The late afternoon sky was cloudless, the wind brisk, the two-lane highway lightly traveled.

Camera dangling from her neck, Jackie studied the North Carolina road map. "Yeah, Currituck." She rested her hand lightly on Laura's thigh. "I'd love to see this region from the air," she said. "Your Aunt Josie was right, sweetheart. These islands do look like a long skinny arm on the map."

"A skeletal arm, Josie called it. See Cape Hatteras? That's the elbow." Laura smiled, enjoying the warm feeling of Jackie's strong hand lightly stroking the fabric of her gray slacks. She closed her hand over Jackie's and squeezed it. "I'll take you there one day. There's a wonderful old brick lighthouse to climb."

Jackie was captivated by Oregon Inlet, its waters dancing with brilliant sunset colors. As they drove onto the bridge, she opened her window, studying the view through her lens. "Just look at this, Laura. It's so incredibly beautiful."

Laura drove more slowly as Jackie's camera clicked and whirred. She glanced at her lover, admiring the short black curls, the strong back. Loving the woman Jackie was.

How incredibly beautiful you are to me, she thought. How good, how loving. She remembered their embrace at San Francisco International Airport a year ago, how they had blocked the flow of passengers like twin rocks in a stream. How Jackie had been so understanding, so patient. Demanding nothing. Just loving her. Leaving her

176

free to find her own feelings. And how glad I am now, Laura said to herself, that I found them.

"So this is the inlet Josie crossed by boat during the hurricane," Jackie said, closing the window and setting aside her camera. She gazed at the lightly rippling red-golden waters. "It looks so calm, so peaceful."

Laura nodded. "It's beautiful. But a deadly piece of water, even when it's calm like this. Constantly shifting currents, hidden sandbars, dangerous shoals everywhere. A lot of people have drowned down there." She thought again about Josie, the illusionary silver path across the water, the beautiful Selene. "Deceptively beautiful," she added.

As they left the bridge, Jackie looked back at the cardboard box in the back seat. "What else did you say was in the box?"

"Oh, some old books. I've hardly glanced at them. Mythology books, mainly. Clarence used them in court." Laura smiled. "He's a super-nice guy. Not to mention a brilliant lawyer. And you'll like Steve, too," she added. She and Jackie had invited Clarence Tate and his lover to spend Sunday with them on Hatteras.

Twilight was rapidly descending as they parked behind the cottage. Noticing that the shutters were open, Laura said with a little laugh, "Bill Tate, bless his heart. Clarence must have phoned him that we were on the way."

"He still has a key?"

"Oh yes! I insisted. He likes being the official watchdog of this house, and *I* like it too."

"What does he think about us, our relationship?" Jackie unloaded their two suitcases.

"He knows you're the most important person in the world to me, and that we're sharing our lives. And that's all he wants to know. He respects our privacy, just as he respects Clarence and Steve's. And so does Dorothy, his wife. They aren't judgmental bigots."

Jackie grinned. "There's hope for the straight world yet."

"With people like Bill and Dorothy Tate in it, there is."

Laura was not surprised to find the oil lamp burning on the kitchen table and the neatly covered pecan pie. "Dorothy's specialty," she explained with a chuckle. "Still warm, too! Bill must have left it here just before we arrived." She was pleasantly surprised to find the fresh block of ice in the ice box, as well as the milk, orange juice, fresh vegetables, and platter of fried chicken. "Now *this,* darling," Laura said with a laugh, "is what's called southern hospitality!"

They entered the living room. Startled, Laura stared at the flame dancing brightly atop the tall creamy candle on the table between the twin windows. Jackie hugged her warmly from behind. "What a nice romantic gesture," she whispered in the twilight-darkened room. "Your sheriff really *has* welcomed us warmly, darling."

Laura shivered slightly, still gazing at the candle.

"I'll build a fire," Jackie said, releasing her.

Laura nodded absently. Why would Tate do this? It was not like him to have forgotten so soon. Surely he would know the candle would only remind her of —

Jackie interrupted her thoughts. "I love this place," she whispered. "So isolated, so cozy." She kissed Laura's neck.

Turning into her arms, Laura murmured, "So you think I shouldn't sell it?"

"No. Never! It's warm, romantic. I feel love in everything I see and touch in this room. Even that crusty old woodstove." She chuckled. "An atmosphere of pure love."

Laura felt it too. She snuggled against Jackie and looked again at the candle. Love, not death, is dancing in that flame, she thought. "To be honest, I don't want to sell it," she said. "But it's on the other side of the continent."

"So what? We can fly here every chance we get. And then retire here when we get to be little old ladies. Or maybe just pull up our stakes before then, and move east."

Laura pulled back and studied her face. "You really like it here that much?"

"I really do. I love your Outer Banks. I'm still a country girl, you know," she added with a grin. "I like tiny little towns and isolated landscapes. And woodfires and candlelight and —"

"But what about our careers?" Laura interrupted.

"What's to keep us from relocating them?"

"Here? But darling, I don't think there's a single clinic on all of these —"

"Not *here*," Jackie laughed. "But maybe in the Norfolk area. We could live there and drive down here on weekends."

"You really *are* serious, aren't you?" Laura studied her with pleased surprise.

Jackie shrugged. "A psychologist with your qualifications and experience . . . You could practice anywhere, Laura."

"But what about your career?"

"Sweetheart, the Tidewater area is crawling with opportunities for me," she said with enthusiasm. "There's NASA in Hampton, and shipyards all over the place. I don't think an electrical engineer could hope for a better spot to look for a new job. Especially an engineer as good as Jacqueline B. Rollins."

"Oh I love you, Jackie B. Rollins!" Laura hugged her tightly. "And we'll talk about it, seriously. Tomorrow."

"Hey, darling, look! There's a full moon. See? Isn't it beautiful?"

For some moments they stood together in silence. The moon hung low above the horizon, its bright beams dancing on the dark water. Laura leaned into Jackie, feeling warm and happy with Jackie's arm around her shoulders.

"Oh, pure serenity," Jackie whispered. "Wasn't it at times like this that your Aunt Josie and her imaginary lover met?"

Laura nodded and glanced down at the brightly burning candle. She sighed, suddenly melancholy. "They were — Josie was enormously happy at times like this," she said softly.

Jackie's arm tightened reassuringly. "Then don't be sad, darling."

"Oh I'm not sad, not about her life. Or even her death, now. But it's a little sad, sometimes, to think about . . . That her body's still —"

"You wish you'd been able to bury her."

"Sometimes. In the family plot. But then again . . ."

"She belongs here," Jackie said softly.

"Yes." She smiled up at her. "Would you get us some wine? In the pantry, darling."

Jackie kissed her lightly and left.

Laura walked about the room, fondly studying its familiar objects — the old couch, the bookcases, the roll-top desk. Everything looked spotlessly clean, recently dusted. She smiled. Dorothy Tate's work, no doubt.

She returned to the windows and stared out at the moonlit beach. She saw two people walking hand in hand near the surf's edge. Surprised that anyone would be there, she looked at them curiously.

The two were dark silhouettes against the glittering moonlight, one in slacks and the other in a long gown that billowed in the breeze. She thought at first they were a man and a woman. But when they turned their backs to the sea and began walking in her direction, she saw they were both women, the one in slacks about her size, with short dark hair. The long pale hair of her companion blew about lightly.

The women neared the beach stairs to the cottage. Laura drew in her breath sharply, stared at them wide-eyed. At the foot of the stairs they paused, looked in her direction, waved.

Her mouth flew open. "It can't be, it *can't!*" she cried. "Jackie! Jackie!" she shouted.

"What is it?" Jackie ran to her side.

"Look! Out there!"

"What?"

Laura paled and seized Jackie's arm. "I — I —" she stammered, "I — don't know." She stared amazed at the empty beach.

Jackie hugged her tightly. "What is it, darling?" she asked anxiously.

Laura shook her head, trembling, and buried her face in her lover's neck. Jackie stroked her hair and rocked her in her arms. "Sweetheart, what's wrong?"

Laura felt the blood returning to her face. After a moment she pulled back, stared silently at the deserted moonlit beach, and then laughed uneasily.

"Sweetheart, what is it?" Jackie asked with a tense smile.

"It's . . . It's nothing, I guess." She smiled up at her weakly. "Just my imagination."

Jackie drew her back into her strong gentle arms. She whispered, "You scared me there for a minute, darling." She chuckled and kissed Laura's brow. "You were so pale, my love . . . As if you'd seen a ghost . . ."

A few of the publications of
THE NAIAD PRESS, INC.
P.O. Box 10543 ● Tallahassee, Florida 32302
Phone (904) 539-9322
Mail orders welcome. Please include 15% postage.

OCTOBER OBSESSION by Meredith More. Josie's rich, secret
Lesbian life.   ISBN 0-941483-18-5 $8.95

HIGH CONTRAST by Jessie Lattimore. 264 pp. Women of the
Crystal Palace.   ISBN 0-941483-17-7   8.95

LESBIAN CROSSROADS by Ruth Baetz. 276 pp. Contemporary
Lesbian lives.   ISBN 0-941483-21-5   9.95

BEFORE STONEWALL: THE MAKING OF A GAY AND
LESBIAN COMMUNITY by Andrea Weiss & Greta Schiller.
96 pp., 25 illus.   ISBN 0-941483-20-7   7.95

WE WALK THE BACK OF THE TIGER by Patricia A. Murphy.
192 pp. Romantic Lesbian novel/beginning women's movement.
                                       ISBN 0-941483-13-4   8.95

SUNDAY'S CHILD by Joyce Bright. 216 pp. Lesbian athletics, at
last the novel about sports.   ISBN 0-941483-12-6   8.95

OSTEN'S BAY by Zenobia N. Vole. 204 pp. Sizzling adventure
romance set on Bonaire.   ISBN 0-941483-15-0   8.95

LESSONS IN MURDER by Claire McNab. 216 pp. 1st in a stylish
mystery series.   ISBN 0-941483-14-2   8.95

YELLOWTHROAT by Penny Hayes. 240 pp. Margarita, bandit,
kidnaps Julia.   ISBN 0-941483-10-X   8.95

SAPPHISTRY: THE BOOK OF LESBIAN SEXUALITY by
Pat Califia. 3d edition, revised. 208 pp.   ISBN 0-941483-24-X   8.95

CHERISHED LOVE by Evelyn Kennedy. 192 pp. Erotic
Lesbian love story.   ISBN 0-941483-08-8   8.95

LAST SEPTEMBER by Helen R. Hull. 208 pp. Six stories & a
glorious novella.   ISBN 0-941483-09-6   8.95

THE SECRET IN THE BIRD by Camarin Grae. 312 pp. Striking,
psychological suspense novel.   ISBN 0-941483-05-3   8.95

TO THE LIGHTNING by Catherine Ennis. 208 pp. Romantic
Lesbian 'Robinson Crusoe' adventure.   ISBN 0-941483-06-1   8.95

THE OTHER SIDE OF VENUS by Shirley Verel. 224 pp.
Luminous, romantic love story.   ISBN 0-941483-07-X   8.95

DREAMS AND SWORDS by Katherine V. Forrest. 192 pp.
Romantic, erotic, imaginative stories. ISBN 0-941483-03-7   8.95

MEMORY BOARD by Jane Rule. 336 pp. Memorable novel about an aging Lesbian couple.   ISBN 0-941483-02-9   8.95

THE ALWAYS ANONYMOUS BEAST by Lauren Wright Douglas. 224 pp. A Caitlin Reese mystery. First in a series.   ISBN 0-941483-04-5   8.95

SEARCHING FOR SPRING by Patricia A. Murphy. 224 pp. Novel about the recovery of love.   ISBN 0-941483-00-2   8.95

DUSTY'S QUEEN OF HEARTS DINER by Lee Lynch. 240 pp. Romantic blue-collar novel.   ISBN 0-941483-01-0   8.95

PARENTS MATTER by Ann Muller. 240 pp. Parents' relationships with Lesbian daughters and gay sons.   ISBN 0-930044-91-6   9.95

THE PEARLS by Shelley Smith. 176 pp. Passion and fun in the Caribbean sun.   ISBN 0-930044-93-2   7.95

MAGDALENA by Sarah Aldridge. 352 pp. Epic Lesbian novel set on three continents.   ISBN 0-930044-99-1   8.95

THE BLACK AND WHITE OF IT by Ann Allen Shockley. 144 pp. Short stories.   ISBN 0-930044-96-7   7.95

SAY JESUS AND COME TO ME by Ann Allen Shockley. 288 pp. Contemporary romance.   ISBN 0-930044-98-3   8.95

LOVING HER by Ann Allen Shockley. 192 pp. Romantic love story.   ISBN 0-930044-97-5   7.95

MURDER AT THE NIGHTWOOD BAR by Katherine V. Forrest. 240 pp. A Kate Delafield mystery. Second in a series.   ISBN 0-930044-92-4   8.95

ZOE'S BOOK by Gail Pass. 224 pp. Passionate, obsessive love story.   ISBN 0-930044-95-9   7.95

WINGED DANCER by Camarin Grae. 228 pp. Erotic Lesbian adventure story.   ISBN 0-930044-88-6   8.95

PAZ by Camarin Grae. 336 pp. Romantic Lesbian adventurer with the power to change the world.   ISBN 0-930044-89-4   8.95

SOUL SNATCHER by Camarin Grae. 224 pp. A puzzle, an adventure, a mystery — Lesbian romance.   ISBN 0-930044-90-8   8.95

THE LOVE OF GOOD WOMEN by Isabel Miller. 224 pp. Long-awaited new novel by the author of the beloved *Patience and Sarah*.   ISBN 0-930044-81-9   8.95

THE HOUSE AT PELHAM FALLS by Brenda Weathers. 240 pp. Suspenseful Lesbian ghost story.   ISBN 0-930044-79-7   7.95

HOME IN YOUR HANDS by Lee Lynch. 240 pp. More stories from the author of *Old Dyke Tales*.   ISBN 0-930044-80-0   7.95

EACH HAND A MAP by Anita Skeen. 112 pp. Real-life poems that touch us all.   ISBN 0-930044-82-7   6.95

SURPLUS by Sylvia Stevenson. 342 pp. A classic early Lesbian
novel.   ISBN 0-930044-78-9   6.95

PEMBROKE PARK by Michelle Martin. 256 pp. Derring-do
and daring romance in Regency England.   ISBN 0-930044-77-0   7.95

THE LONG TRAIL by Penny Hayes. 248 pp. Vivid adventures
of two women in love in the old west.   ISBN 0-930044-76-2   8.95

HORIZON OF THE HEART by Shelley Smith. 192 pp. Hot
romance in summertime New England.   ISBN 0-930044-75-4   7.95

AN EMERGENCE OF GREEN by Katherine V. Forrest. 288
pp. Powerful novel of sexual discovery.   ISBN 0-930044-69-X   8.95

THE LESBIAN PERIODICALS INDEX edited by Claire
Potter. 432 pp. Author & subject index.   ISBN 0-930044-74-6   29.95

DESERT OF THE HEART by Jane Rule. 224 pp. A classic;
basis for the movie *Desert Hearts*.   ISBN 0-930044-73-8   7.95

SPRING FORWARD/FALL BACK by Sheila Ortiz Taylor.
288 pp. Literary novel of timeless love. ISBN 0-930044-70-3   7.95

FOR KEEPS by Elisabeth Nonas. 144 pp. Contemporary novel
about losing and finding love.   ISBN 0-930044-71-1   7.95

TORCHLIGHT TO VALHALLA by Gale Wilhelm. 128 pp.
Classic novel by a great Lesbian writer. ISBN 0-930044-68-1   7.95

LESBIAN NUNS: BREAKING SILENCE edited by Rosemary
Curb and Nancy Manahan. 432 pp. Unprecedented autobiographies
of religious life.   ISBN 0-930044-62-2   9.95

THE SWASHBUCKLER by Lee Lynch. 288 pp. Colorful novel
set in Greenwich Village in the sixties. ISBN 0-930044-66-5   8.95

MISFORTUNE'S FRIEND by Sarah Aldridge. 320 pp. Historical Lesbian novel set on two continents. ISBN 0-930044-67-3   7.95

A STUDIO OF ONE'S OWN by Ann Stokes. Edited by
Dolores Klaich. 128 pp. Autobiography.   ISBN 0-930044-64-9   7.95

SEX VARIANT WOMEN IN LITERATURE by Jeannette
Howard Foster. 448 pp. Literary history. ISBN 0-930044-65-7   8.95

A HOT-EYED MODERATE by Jane Rule. 252 pp. Hard-hitting
essays on gay life; writing; art.   ISBN 0-930044-57-6   7.95

INLAND PASSAGE AND OTHER STORIES by Jane Rule.
288 pp. Wide-ranging new collection.   ISBN 0-930044-56-8   7.95

WE TOO ARE DRIFTING by Gale Wilhelm. 128 pp. Timeless
Lesbian novel, a masterpiece.   ISBN 0-930044-61-4   6.95

AMATEUR CITY by Katherine V. Forrest. 224 pp. A Kate
Delafield mystery. First in a series.   ISBN 0-930044-55-X   7.95

THE SOPHIE HOROWITZ STORY by Sarah Schulman. 176
pp. Engaging novel of madcap intrigue.   ISBN 0-930044-54-1   7.95

THE BURNTON WIDOWS by Vickie P. McConnell. 272 pp. A
Nyla Wade mystery, second in the series. ISBN 0-930044-52-5 7.95

OLD DYKE TALES by Lee Lynch. 224 pp. Extraordinary
stories of our diverse Lesbian lives. ISBN 0-930044-51-7 7.95

DAUGHTERS OF A CORAL DAWN by Katherine V. Forrest.
240 pp. Novel set in a Lesbian new world. ISBN 0-930044-50-9 7.95

THE PRICE OF SALT by Claire Morgan. 288 pp. A milestone
novel, a beloved classic. ISBN 0-930044-49-5 8.95

AGAINST THE SEASON by Jane Rule. 224 pp. Luminous,
complex novel of interrelationships. ISBN 0-930044-48-7 8.95

LOVERS IN THE PRESENT AFTERNOON by Kathleen
Fleming. 288 pp. A novel about recovery and growth.
ISBN 0-930044-46-0 8.95

TOOTHPICK HOUSE by Lee Lynch. 264 pp. Love between
two Lesbians of different classes. ISBN 0-930044-45-2 7.95

MADAME AURORA by Sarah Aldridge. 256 pp. Historical
novel featuring a charismatic "seer." ISBN 0-930044-44-4 7.95

CURIOUS WINE by Katherine V. Forrest. 176 pp. Passionate
Lesbian love story, a best-seller. ISBN 0-930044-43-6 8.95

BLACK LESBIAN IN WHITE AMERICA by Anita Cornwell.
141 pp. Stories, essays, autobiography. ISBN 0-930044-41-X 7.50

CONTRACT WITH THE WORLD by Jane Rule. 340 pp.
Powerful, panoramic novel of gay life. ISBN 0-930044-28-2 7.95

YANTRAS OF WOMANLOVE by Tee A. Corinne. 64 pp.
Photos by noted Lesbian photographer. ISBN 0-930044-30-4 6.95

MRS. PORTER'S LETTER by Vicki P. McConnell. 224 pp.
The first Nyla Wade mystery. ISBN 0-930044-29-0 7.95

TO THE CLEVELAND STATION by Carol Anne Douglas.
192 pp. Interracial Lesbian love story. ISBN 0-930044-27-4 6.95

THE NESTING PLACE by Sarah Aldridge. 224 pp. A
three-woman triangle—love conquers all! ISBN 0-930044-26-6 7.95

THIS IS NOT FOR YOU by Jane Rule. 284 pp. A letter to a
beloved is also an intricate novel. ISBN 0-930044-25-8 8.95

FAULTLINE by Sheila Ortiz Taylor. 140 pp. Warm, funny,
literate story of a startling family. ISBN 0-930044-24-X 6.95

These are just a few of the many Naiad Press titles — we are the oldest and
largest lesbian/feminist publishing company in the world. Please request a
complete catalog. We offer personal service; we encourage and welcome
direct mail orders from individuals who have limited access to bookstores
carrying our publications.